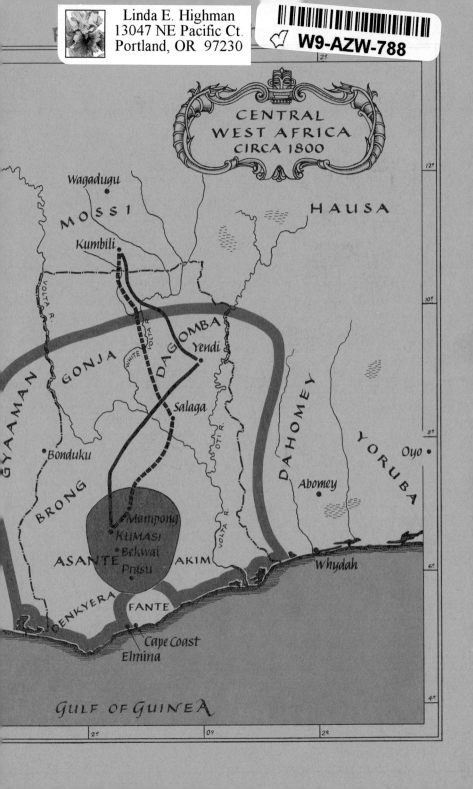

CENTRAL WEST AFRICA CIRCA 1800

MOSSI

HAUSA

Wagadugu

Kumbili

GYAMAN

GONJA

VOLTA R.

WHITE VOLTA R.

DAGOMBA

Yendi

Salaga

OTI R.

DAHOMEY

YORUBA

Oyo

Bonduku

BRONG

ASANTE

Mampong

KUMASI

Bekwai

Prasu

AKIM

VOLTA R.

Abomey

Whydah

DENKYERA

FANTE

Cape Coast

Elmina

GULF OF GUINEA

The Return

THE RETURN

A Novel

BY
YAW M. BOATENG

PANTHEON BOOKS, NEW YORK

For my grandmother,
Akosua Kyem

First American Edition

Copyright © 1977 by Yaw M. Boateng

All rights reserved under International and Pan-American Copyright Conventions. Published in the United States by Pantheon Books, a division of Random House, Inc., New York, and simultaneously in Canada by Random House of Canada Limited, Toronto. Originally published in Great Britain by Heinemann Educational Books Ltd., London.

Library of Congress Cataloging in Publication Data

Boateng, Yaw M., 1950–.

The Return.
I. Title.
PZ4.B6623Re3 [PR9379.9.B6]   823   77-5018
ISBN 0-394-41724-0

Manufactured in the United States of America

INTRODUCTION

For four centuries, millions of Africans were wrenched from their native lands and transported mainly to the Americas to become slaves. Yet the effects on Africa itself of this unparalleled uprooting have been largely ignored. Slave trade routes have been traced, the motives of the slavers analyzed, and the experiences of the slaves in their new homelands carefully depicted. Even today, however, most people have only the vaguest idea of the wars, the conflict, and the destruction that took place among those Africans the slave trade left behind. *The Return* is their story.

The Return focuses on a world in which, to remain free, one had to enslave; a time when all of West Africa obeyed one simple law: sell or be sold. To sell meant to obtain arms from the white slave traders; not to sell meant military inferiority and enslavement by others. As a result, those people who cooperated with the Western slave traders often became the powerful African kingdoms and empires of that time. Such a kingdom was Asante, the heart of this book and one of the most powerful slave empires ever to arise in Africa. Within a few decades of its birth in the late seventeeth century, its armies of trained musketeers had swept all before them, establishing control over most of modern Ghana, as well as large chunks of Togo and the Ivory Coast.

The Return picks up the story of the Asante around 1800, when they were at the peak of their power. This was a crucial moment in African history. With the overseas slave markets becoming glutted, the Europeans were beginning to realize that control over the entire land of Africa would be much more profitable than tinning up and shipping off a few million slaves to the Americas. This shift away from slavery threatened to pull the props out from under the Asante Empire. After generations of dependence on trading slaves for arms,

v

Asante would not give in lightly to such a formula for military and political collapse. A clash with the West was inevitable.

With the possible exception of the Zulus in southern Africa, no other black African people resisted European colonization so fiercely, so courageously, or so successfully. The first major British military expedition against the Asante in 1824 turned into a Western nightmare. An army of crack troops was totally defeated by the much-underestimated Asante sharpshooters armed with Danish guns. It took another fifty years before the British finally seized and burned Kumasi, the royal capital, to ashes. Even as late as 1900, the Asante, led by a woman named Yaa Asantewaa, rose in a last bloody rebellion. Their defeat and the massacre of Asante warriors broke the spirit of the nation. They never fought the British again.

For the American reader of *The Return,* a small amount of background information may be useful. In the first millenium A.D., the Almoravid Moslems (of modern Morocco and Mauritania) set out on a series of holy wars, occupying Spain and parts of modern France. In 1076, they extended their conquests southward across the Sahara, setting off a series of forced migrations all over West Africa. Among those who fled the Moslems were the terribly weak Akan-speaking people, who finally settled in the thick coastal forests of Central West Africa. For a few generations, as they mixed with the peoples already settled there, a kind of peace prevailed. Then the European ships began to arrive off the coast.

The Europeans did not, in fact, introduce slavery to Africa. It had been an ancient custom there, though it never took the brutal form later developed in the Americas. The slave in Africa, while not free, belonged not so much *to* as *with* a particular family. As a result, African history is filled with stories of slaves who rose to important posts. Sakora, the freed slave who ruled the West African kingdom of Mali, is but one example.

At first, the coastal Akans were quite willing to give their European visitors slaves to serve them. Later, as the demand increased and they observed the Europeans' brutal treatment of slaves, the Akans were no longer willing to give away their own household slaves. Instead, they began hunting among weaker groups further inland for

vi

slaves to exchange for the whisky, guns, and beads to which they had become addicted.

Suddenly and dramatically, out of this situation, arose the Asante Empire. Initially, it was only a union of inland Akan clans formed expressly for a war of liberation from the Denkyira, a powerful slave-trading Akan group nearer the coast. Indeed, the word "Asante" itself derives from *Osa nit*—"because of war." Asante not only won the war but soon replaced the Denkyira as one of the most terrible slave empires in history.

Actually, Asante was only one of several attempts by exploited inland peoples to break free. Most of these attempts failed, as the peoples nearer the cost had better access to the guns of the Western slave traders. The Asante, however, succeeded beyond their wildest dreams, conquering numerous Akan and non-Akan kingdoms in the process. Indeed, some of these conquered states, with far more brilliant pasts than the Akans, were turned into humble slave-and-tribute paying subject states, their cultural development arrested by the Asante musketeer armies. Gonja, which plays a key role in this book, was one of these.

It was the gun provided by the slave traders that gave Asante its superiority. Originally, the Asante army had fought with the traditional bow and arrow, spear and sword, but soon the musket and strict military discipline enabled Asante to whip kingdoms far bigger than itself. Naturally, Asante took great pains that none of its subject states should receive enough Western arms to become a serious threat, though—as you will see—they were not always successful. Certain peoples, especially those nearer the coast, frequently rebelled and had to be put down in costly wars. Each of the small city-states which originally made up the empire was expected to supply men for the Asante army. As other states were conquered, they were increasingly requested to do the same. Like the hero of this novel, many men from among those conquered people rose to important military posts.

As the empire grew, it became less and less possible to maintain unity and subservience through terror alone. So Asante's shrewd leaders began to use the Islamic religion of some of its subject states as a means of imperial control. They had noticed that truly zealous Moslems put religious loyalties above tribal loyalties. So trustworthy Imams—religious leaders—were brought to the capital to serve as record-keepers and "workers of charms." Yet, perhaps remembering that Moslem holy wars had driven them to the coastal forests and into the arms of the white slavers, the Asante maintained a deep fear and distrust of Islam. In fact, one Asante king, mentioned in the novel, was promptly deposed when he moved from simply using the religion to openly accepting it as his own.

Seku and Jakpa, the two central figures in *The Return,* are not Asante but come from the subject state of Gonja. After a separation of several years, they meet again in Kumasi, the Asante capital, where each, unknown to the other, has made his way into an important post in the service of the king—one as a fierce warrior in the Asante army, the other as a Moslem record-keeper. There, the two men are inevitably brought face-to-face with the fact that they are both working for an empire whose smallest advance depends upon the further degeneration of their once-proud people.

With the exception of the main characters, who are fictitious, and the small tribe I call the Kakris, which is equally so, *The Return* is based on historical facts. The more bizarre or incredible a statement might appear, the less likely that it was fabricated by the author. In fact, though the name "Kakri" is made up, any person who knows West Africa well will be able to call to mind a dozen or so similarly weak tribes which were preyed upon so often by the slave trade that they fell into complete degeneration: cannibalism and incest, among other customs. Many Westerners still attribute such practices to all Africans, when they normally applied only to the worst victims of the slave trade. I hope *The Return* will help to remind its readers of the magnitude of the disaster the Western slavers' arrival proved for Africa as a whole. It is easily forgotten today how many of modern Africa's problems stem not just from its ninety-year experience with European colonialism, but from the centuries of havoc wreaked by the slave trade.

—YAW M. BOATENG

I

When Seku Wattara first told his wife of his intentions to join the Kambonse Regiment, she couldn't believe her ears. This was nearly four years ago. He had killed a man. He hadn't meant to, of course. It was during a Kokoa wrestling tournament, and his opponent had been undefeated champion for five years. It was Seku's hardest fight. He could barely stand upright as the yellow Fulani fell down for a last time and lay still. Seku did not understand his wife's protests: he really had no choice. The Fulanis, led by the dead wrestler's elder brother Siaka, wanted their revenge. His Gonja friends deserted him; he went with three to the wrestling grounds as his seconds, and he returned alone. Only one Asante man, a complete stranger, accompanied him home. His name was Yaw Ntiamoah, a young nobleman of Pataase, near Kumasi, who persuaded the elders to interfere in the affair and force a promise out of the Fulani to allow Seku and his wife to live in peace. Earlier they had refused Seku's offer of a bull as compensation and would not hear of his attending the funeral to show his respect. Once they even sent a man to waylay his wife at the stream, but she escaped. When Seku found out he rushed to the Fulani meat stalls in the main market, blind with anger. Six big Fulanis held him whilst Siaka got a butcher's knife to cut his throat, but he was saved by the asafo warriors, policemen in peacetime, and they took him to see Ntiamoah for verification of his story.

He owed his friend two lives, his own and his wife's. Now Ntiamoah wanted him to join the Kambonse, the special regiment of Dagomba musketeers. He liked the strong Seku, and he knew that as a stranger in Kumasi without any property, it was his best chance of improving his social standing. Ntiamoah was sure from the manners and great beauty of the couple that they were from no mean family in the northern savannahs. What he didn't understand was why they chose to live so poorly – Seku was trapping cutting grass, squirrels and pouched rats for sale in the market when they first met. But he never asked. He liked Seku and wanted to help him, not embarass him. About two months after they met Seku told his wife one evening after supper that he wanted to follow his friend's advice and join the Asante army.

'But why, Seku,' she asked, 'you are no Dagomba but a Gonja, and Gonja and Asante —' she stopped.

He shrugged. 'I was brought up in Mossi. I hardly know Gonja.'

'But Mossi is no friend of Asante's either. That is why your father took shelter there.'

He gave her a quick, annoyed look. 'My father is dead,' he replied. 'I have a right to lead my own life.'

She said nothing to that and began clearing the table. Her meekness annoyed him further.

'Look, Mbinge,' he began, 'I want to forget the past. I can't keep to my father's ideals because I am different and have gone through different experiences and circumstances from him. The Asante conquests destroyed all he had, and the Mossi gave him shelter. I am a refugee from the Mossi, who hunted me like a thief. I have found refuge in Asante, and a friend who can be relied upon. I owe the Mossi nothing.'

'And your people, the Gonja?'

'I hardly know them – indeed I speak Gonja but poorly. You yourself saw how the Gonja young men I befriended in this town fled me even as I got into my first major problem.'

'So you want to punish them by burning their villages?'

Now Seku was on his feet, trembling with rage. 'You are being stupid, Mbinge. I am not interested in killing, but I need the financial means to survive. I am tired of roaming the forests trapping rats, risking snake bite just for a bare pittance to stay alive. If I join the Kambonse my social standing will go up. We can have our own home, with servants if you want, and good land to farm. Can't you see, woman, what we stand to gain?'

'Seku you are blind,' Mbinge sobbed, the tears running down her cheeks. 'You are risking so much. What if you are killed? What will happen to me? I know nobody in this town; you are the only thing I have. If you should go I might as well come with you, because I can't go back to my own people.'

Seku took the bowl from her hand and put it back on the table. He slipped an arm over her shoulders comfortingly. 'I always take care, Mbinge. I promise you I'll always return. Remember the fetish we went to see? They said I'd have a long life. And more, my Asante friend has promised to take care of you should anything happen to me.'

She slipped gently from his arms and began picking up the dishes

2

again. He sighed to himself, thinking it was over, but at the doorway she turned and said, 'I know why you want to go to war, Seku. It may be partly because you are desperate to improve your social status here. But I know as well as you, even if you won't admit it to yourself, that you still think about it, and feel shame and guilt for what happened to him whose name you never mention. That is why you want to make war and kill and be violent, for what you think you should have done that day. I know you were not afraid that day, I know you have never known cowardice, but I know you don't know yourself how brave you are and were. So go and kill, Seku, and show the world your strength and courage. And if you should never come back to me, I can always take a dose of poison.'

She fled sobbing from the room before he could answer. Seku stared long at the disturbed raffia curtain, and in his eyes were pain, uncertainty and fear.

He loved his wife. He had made a great sacrifice to get her, and his conscience worried him. He worried for many days after this discussion. Could he really trust his friend Ntiamoah to take Mbinge back to her home village in Mossi, a journey of many weeks, if he should die at war? He wanted to tell Ntiamoah he had changed his mind. For a week he stayed at home, neglecting his traps. He saw how hard a life she led, cooking, washing, sweeping, carrying heavy wares to and from the market. She was even tilling a small garden of cocoyam, cassava and vegetables. She who was once a princess! No, it couldn't go on like this forever. He went to tell his friend to hurry up with the arrangements. Mbinge never brought up the matter again, but he knew her mind. Despite the pain her silent reproach caused him, he felt a man: he had done the right thing.

Now, less than four years later, he was still very much alive; indeed he was already third in command of the Kambonse Regiment. He was a national hero: he had just returned from the Gyaaman War, where the Mamponghene, commander-in-chief of the campaign, had called him to offer presents and congratulations. He had led the Kambose in a courageous charge just when the Gyase, or Rear Regiment, where the most senior commanders gave out their instructions in relative security, had been surrounded: this was the main reason for his quick promotion. Three weeks later, he again helped lead the Kambonse to rout the main Gyaaman army. This deed made him a hero of the entire army. There were many brave warriors, but Seku especially caught the eye because of his great height amidst the medium-sized Asante, and

3

because he was one of the most handsome men in all Asante.

They moved from their poor quarters in Zongo, the foreigners' quarters, to Aboabo, a relatively new area in Kumasi where most of the King's senior warriors lived with their families. Mbinge now had maids and two strong male servants. She could live her life in relative peace and laziness now, he thought, but instead she chose to sell bean-cakes on market days. Women were strange indeed. He understood her loneliness when he was away, but why didn't she just visit friends instead? She replied that all her friends were busy, hard-working women, so he gave up. Perhaps she adored chatting in the market – let her have her way. She was pregnant after so many years – a pleasant surprise for him.

Toward sunset Mbinge returned and heated some bean-cakes for him. He loved them. He gobbled them up, and she asked him, 'What did they feed you on, Seku? You have lost so much weight.'

'We took food along. But it was never for long periods. When the Asante army marches, scouts are sent forward to all chiefs subservient to Kumasi through whose lands the army will pass. They will be expected to help house and feed the warriors till they leave. Now in our case we had all the chiefs of Asante, Brong and Gonja on our side, and we managed well till we entered Gyaaman territory. Gyaaman is a savannah land even as Mossi is, and the rebels destroyed all farms on their retreat, so that though we had stores of food from Gonja, apart from dried meat it all went foul, and we experienced long periods of hunger.'

'Well, how did you manage?'

'We had gari*, horses from Gonja, dogs, even vultures and sometimes wild berries and fruits. It was a hard campaign, not so much because of the enemy as because of the harshness of the land.'

Mbinge made a wry face at the mention of vultures, and Seku laughed. He wanted to say something else about the war customs of Asante, but he knew it would shock her, so he decided against it. Soon after the Asante army had crossed Gonja to engage in a minor encounter corpses from the battle were sent to the fetish priests who removed the hearts and prepared a magic broth for those fighting for the first time. Seku was fortunate to be spared the broth, because he had already killed, and he appreciated the training he had undergone with Ntiamoah's uncle. The young warriors had drunk eagerly of the broth,

---

* gari: a sort of flour scraped from cassava and then roasted. It lasts for months and is edible without further preparation.

4

but Seku had seen many sneak into the bushes to vomit afterwards.

The servants set water for them in the bathing place, and one fetched a torch as it was getting dark. They didn't consider it odd that the two should bath together, but only because they were used to it. In the Asante society at large it would have been considered quite abnormal.

Ever since his return to Kumasi a week before, Seku bathed at least once a day with his wife, usually in the evening. In the mornings he slept on while she prepared to go to market. On the very first evening of his arrival he had expressed this wish. She had not immediately understood why: it was the first time since the first months of their marriage that he had shown this desire. Now, of course, she knew what to expect. As soon as the raffia curtains of the bathroom were closed, he helped her undress quickly but gently, and went on one knee and put an ear against her stomach. He giggled boyishly each time the baby kicked in its mother's womb, and she pushed her fingers into his stiff curly hair and scratched the scalp fondly. His big soft hands were a contrast to his hard body, and each time they touched her she felt some regret that she was pregnant. Now he rubbed his chest, back and stomach gently against her belly, and as he stood up she saw that his pieto was oddly distended in front, but he had pushed back his bottom so as to avoid contact of that part of his body with hers. Poor Seku, she thought. It was obviously so hard for him. Men bore the restraint much worse than women, particularly when they had just returned from war.

'Take another wife, Seku,' she said for the tenth time since his return.

He looked down at himself, then adjusted his 'pieto', pushing the thing between his legs. But even as he turned up his head to smile triumphantly, it sprang out again.

Mbinge did not smile. 'I mean it, Seku. It is not fair for either of us. Your friends laugh at you because you keep only one wife, and the women look strangely at me and whisper behind my back that I am a witch.'

Seku gave up the experiment with his pants and removed the pieto, and he lay it on top of Mbinge's own clothes which she had hung on the line keeping the raffia curtains in place. It suddenly occured to him that the servants in the courtyard might see something, but no, the curtain was too high. He still made no reply.

'Seku,' Mbinge went on in the same serious voice, 'it is a thing of the past. It is over and done with. Don't torture yourself.'

'I made a vow, Mbinge,' he replied at last. 'I don't break vows.'

5

She felt the tears coming to her eyes, and she checked herself with an effort. When she spoke her voice was calm and even. 'You are not fair, Seku. What do you think I feel, that you should use me as a thing to swear oaths on?'

Now he was looking earnestly at her. 'I love you, Mbinge,' he said, holding her shoulders with his hands. 'I swear I do. I swear I have no desire for any other woman. I sacrificed a lot to get you, and I know you have lost greatly in coming with me. But I do not understand. In the beginning before we married, you were proud and wanted me for yourself alone. Now that I have vowed to be yours alone, you are unhappy, and would like to see me on top of another woman. What is going wrong with this world?'

'I love you as only the truest woman can love the most gallant of men, Seku,' she replied, 'and the gods know I would be jealous enough to see you hold hands with another woman. But, Seku, it is different when you decide something in freedom as when you feel compelled to do it. In the beginning you kept me for yourself alone, but even since the night of the vow I can't be so sure whether your love is for my sake, or if a large part of it is a forced determination to keep your vow.'

He looked at her and his eyes became sad. He turned to face the wall. 'My mind wanders back to the campaign. I see the many fires lit at night, so that to a scout on a horse on a hill the whole plain seems like the sky itself, with its own kind of stars. I see the warriors scrambling awake to the drums at dawn, I see them checking their guns, swords, bows and spears. My ears are filled with the sound of drumming – the Mamponghene, commander-in-chief of the campaign, sending out his orders to the various regiments in a code which is changed every two days so that the enemy cannot learn to decipher it. Now we are closing ranks with the enemy, and the air is filled with war-cries, gun-fire, the cling of metal, and the special war horns, flutes and drums which serve to bring confusion among the enemy ranks. I see the Asante army in difficulties, the generals are sweating, and they spit out red kola from their mouths. Now the Kambonse charges, and the enemy gives way. They are routed, and the way to Bonduku, capital of Gyaaman, is open. I remember the agreements on the terms of surrender, the many arrests made. I see the Asante warriors being entertained with feasts and lovely laughing girls of Gyaaman. My friends laugh and forget themselves; only the generals keep aloof as they scramble for juicy flesh to enjoy. I feel a hot desire too, but it is not for them.'

Now he turned to look at her. 'It is not just the vow, Mbinge. It is

6

something else called love. But the vow does help to keep me strong and faithful.'

She felt the tears coming, and she threw herself at his mighty chest with a cry. He held her in silence till the sobbing subsided, and then she whispered, 'I am so happy, Seku, but so afraid.'

Two days later Ntiamoah came to visit them. He was troubled, because Opoku II, the new King of Asante was very sick. He had succeeded Osei Kwame, who had been destooled. Ntiamoah told Seku that if Opoku died, Osei Kwame might plunge the nation into another war in his efforts to regain the monarchy. Though Osei was disliked in Kumasi, his popularity among the Moslem subject states to the north was so great that some might declare war on Kumasi just as Gyaaman had done.

'I do not fear for Asante,' Seku replied quickly. 'Asante troops are the most disciplined in this part of the world.'

'I agree, my brother.' Ntiamoah looked rather strangely at Seku. 'These are not nations capable of breaking Asante. But I think of the unnecessary bloodshed, I think of the tears of the women of Gonja, I think of the problems you yourself will encounter. Think again, my brother from Gonja. It will be no easy task for you to lead a regiment into the land of your own people.'

Seku was looking at the floor. His wife and best friend waited, looking at the strong, confused man. He made no reply.

*   *   *

Eighteen months passed between the day Seku told Ntiamoah of his wishes to become a warrior in the army and the day he finally was enrolled as a member of the Kambonse Regiment. After long talks with each other, both he and Ntiamoah agreed that the Kambonse offered the best possibilities for a non-Asante, so they went to see Ntiamoah's uncle Amankwa Abinowa for help to give Seku an appointment. The old warrior listened, but he thought it would be better if Seku first got some experience elsewhere, as the Kambonse was one of the toughest regiments, and was often sent to the hottest parts during a battle. He therefore contacted the Gyaasehene, the King's treasurer, and Seku was sent to Prasu as one of the guards of Kusi Manu, a tax collector.

He was there for nearly a year, returning to Kumasi every four months for a week when the official came to give a report to the Gyaasehene. He learnt a lot about Asante customs as he accompanied the official everywhere, including visits to the elders and priests of the

7

town. Prasu was a bordertown in the sense that it marked a division between the true Asante and their subjects the Denkyera, the same people who had once been their masters. All traders from many lands, especially those of the Fante, in whose land the white men of the Great Sea had built many castles and harbours, came to see Kusi Manu when they crossed the river Pra into Asante territory, and he told them the laws of Kumasi concerning the proportion of their goods which belonged to the King by custom.

When the tax-collector returned to Kumasi for a third time, Abinowa questioned him about Seku's progress. What he heard must have pleased him, because he sent for Seku and told him, 'Young man, you have told me you want to be a warrior. You have learnt to use the gun, which is our supreme weapon. You have been a personal bodyguard for some months, and you have had some insight into Asante life. It is still too early for you to join the Kambonse, because you have no experience in warfare. You will not accompany the tax-collector when he returns to Prasu. An opportunity has risen for you to gain further experience. You will accompany me as a body-guard to Bekwai. The Bekwaihene, chief of Bekwai, has sent word to Kumasi that he needs help. Many peasants have rebelled against the tax laws of Bekwai, and the chief believes that large troops will be needed to frighten them into subservience. Like all other Asante states, Bekwai has its own army, but it may have to fight and shed blood before the peasants will give in.'

In Bekwai, Seku shot his first man. It was in the market place, and he was with Abinowa and Ntiamoah, who had accompanied his uncle. Abinowa was having an earnest discussion with one of the peasants who had come to sell in the market. Most of the other peasants no longer came to the market, and Abinowa was telling this particular seller the importance of settling one's differences calmly without having to resort to painful boycotts. According to Asante tradition since Osei Tutu's time, even the Asantehene could not interfere in the internal affairs of any component state, but the Bekwaihene was desperate, and he would listen to advice from Kumasi to make things easier for the farmers. A number of the rebelling peasants had been shouting insults at the Kumasi warriors, and then suddenly one of them began upsetting the wares of the other traders. This was a little too much. Abinowa snapped an order at Seku, and Seku took careful aim and fired. The man spun like a top and fell, and the other rebels went back, afraid. Abinowa went forward and addressed them, saying:

8

'Children of Bekwai, we are all Asantefo. Bekwai was a founding state of Asante, and many of her sons have fought to bring glory to our land. The people of Bekwai belong to the same Oyoko clan as the Asantehene and traditional sons of Kumasi. Otumfuor has sent us his warriors only at the request of your chief, the Bekwaihene. We have spoken with him, and he is prepared to talk the matter over with representatives you will send. He is even prepared to let some of us from Kumasi sit down with you as observers to ensure that justice is done. Stop your violent protests. It will do you no good to contest Otumfuor with force. It is Otumfuor's wish that you settle your differences calmly, without bloodshed.'

Seku went to inspect the body of the man he had shot, and he saw how horribly effective the gun was in causing death. A hole big enough for him to shove his hand in had been blasted in the head so that the face was no more recognisable. There was blood everywhere, a deep bright red mingled with white bits of brain. An old woman was weeping because all her pineapples, oranges and yams were soaked in blood and could no longer be sold. The man had been wearing a greyish cloth, not well made, and he had been unarmed. The legs seemed to have been those of a young person, perhaps only a boy. Seku felt awkward, and when Ntiamoah congratulated him on his marksmanship, he turned quickly away.

They remained for four months in Bekwai. There were two minor clashes between the Kumasi troops and the rebels, and in both Seku displayed great calmness and courage: he was a naturally gifted warrior. During the second clash the elders nearly ordered the men to open fire, but as the peasants carried only sticks, stones and poorly made cutlasses and knives, Nana Abinowa suggested that the youngest warriors be sent against them as an exercise. Seku captured one of their most important leaders and sent him to the elders.

The elders held a number of conferences and meetings to discuss the problem, and after the capture of their leader, the rebels were ready to come to terms. Neither Seku nor Ntiamoah ever attended any of these meetings, and even old Abinowa and the other Kumasi elders who went acted only as observers and were careful not to interfere in the discussions.

        *   *   *

Seku remembered the Gyaaman war, which had made him famous. It was Ntiamoah who came personally to warn his friend to prepare for war. By this time Seku had been many months in the Kambonse, but

9

since there were no wars or rebels, he had stayed at home most of the time.

'Prepare, brother Seku,' he said. 'My uncle has received word to gather his warriors. All other regiments have received these instructions, and we shall march within a week. The Mamponghene will meet the main army at the Offin river to lead it against the rebels.'

'Will you fight as well?' Seku asked.

'Yes, my brother. I shall march with my uncle in the Adonteng. Since Kambonse is also a frontal regiment, we shall be near each other.'

After Ntiamoah had left Mbinge came to see her husband. She had overheard their conversation, and her heart was heavy. Seku sat her on his lap and caressed her, but she didn't respond. She took his gun and polished it carefully and checked his pellets and gunpowder. When they lay in bed to sleep, she suggested they see some fetish priests to pray and to make offerings. He readily agreed. He had not yet seen the power of Asante fetishes, and he was curious to hear what they would predict. But when Mbinge asked him to see a Moslem Imam as well, Seku's face clouded over.

'I am through with Moslems, Mbinge,' he replied. 'I do not believe in their powers. I prefer the fetishes of Asante and of other people, but don't discuss Moslems with me. I don't understand why you, a woman of Mossi, should be so fascinated by these men. The gods of Mossi are more powerful than their Allah, whom I call the helpless.'

* * *

Ntiamoah was celebrating. He had invited several people to attend, and promised plenty to eat and even more to drink. As they neared the building, Seku nodded at his two companions and smiled. They were making a racket inside – there was much drumming, blowing of horns and singing, almost as if it were a public durbar organised by some important chief. But he was glad that they were making so much noise, because Ntiamoah had moved house and gone to a different place with more space, and without the music he might not have found it so quickly. He paused a few moments to inspect the front view of the house and couldn't help noting that it was the most attractive building in the street. It had a much higher wall than Ntiamoah's old house, and even in the light of the setting sun it was clearly in much better repair. He pounded at the door and a young man opened it.

'Welcome, Nana,' he said, addressing Seku as 'Grandfather', the most honourable way of naming people of high standing in Asante society.

Seku and his two men entered and looked at the spectacle, trying to figure out where Ntiamoah was. In the centre of the courtyard was a number of dancers performing to the music, which was supplied by a largish band playing at one end. Seku remembered his first impressions of Asante dancing; he had admired the graceful 'adwoa' very much, but it was only much later that he had come to understand that though adwoa could be danced just for merriment, most of the time when professional dancers performed, they were enacting a drama of some sort. Today the men were trying to seduce the women, but they threw away the handkerchiefs of their suitors and turned proudly away. The men picked them up and tried again, dancing a different style. Again and again their approaches were rejected, till, just when he thought he could predict all actions, the women finally gave in, and joined the men in dancing a marriage dance. There were many loud claps and rude shouts as this occurred, and Seku thought, the guests must really be drunk.

One of Seku's bodyguards pointed and said, 'There he is.'

Ntiamoah was sitting on a high cushion with a look of mock self-importance which caused Seku to smile. He knew that his friend did it as an imitation of the Ya Na King of Dagomba, about whom Ntiamoah often made jokes to his friends. Seku saw that at his feet was a large pot of palm wine, and Ntiamoah was using it as a table for his calabash, no doubt to prevent other men helping him. Beautiful young girls sat on either side of him, and one behind him, but Seku couldn't make out where any of his wives were.

One of Ntiamoah's girl-friends pointed as they made their way through the dancers, and he rose to welcome them.

'My brother Seku,' he said as he embraced him, 'you are late. I was thinking of sending men to drag you here.'

Ntiamoah pushed away one of the girls and pulled a seat for him at his side. Seku nodded at his men, and they went to see if they could make friends with some of the many young dancers with warm thighs.

A girl brought Seku some roasted meat, cut into little pieces all pierced and held in place by a narrow stick. He thanked her absentmindedly, and only when she was gone did he realise she was the reason for Ntiamoah's party.

'I am sorry, Yaw,' he apologised, 'I didn't notice her.'

'What?' Ntiamoah asked, puzzled.

'I mean, your wife just came by, and I didn't say my greetings.'

'You mean Amina?'

'Yes.'

'Oh, forget it, the wedding is over.' Ntiamoah poured out some wine for his colleague.

Seku's surprised look only amused him. 'My brother,' he laughed, 'I paid a fortune for the girl's bride-price, and I have a right to enjoy her services now. True, it is because of her I make this feast, but she must begin sometime to learn the place of woman.' He laughed again and pinched the bottom of one of his female admirers.

Seku smiled at him and shook his head. Amina was from Gonja. During the campaign against the Gyaaman, the Asante army had camped in a Gonja town, and there Ntiamoah had seen the girl, and made his approaches. When they left the town to engage the Gyaaman, Ntiamoah troubled Seku greatly with his fears that he might never see the girl again, and with the defeat of Gyaaman, he had asked for permission to visit her, naturally with Seku. Her father, an old wrinkled man, had put two and two together – the Asante victory and Ntiamoah's obvious high standing in the Asante army – and demanded a very high bride-price. Ntiamoah and Seku had counted what they had in between them; it wasn't enough, so they had to ask the Asante generals for a loan. Seku could still remember Ntiamoah saying, 'My brother, once I did you a turn. Now is a chance to repay me. The generals have great admiration for you, and if you should come with me to plead on my behalf, I have no doubt my fears will be over, and we shall enter Kumasi with this pearl of Gonja.' Hardly a month had passed since the grand wedding in Gonja, but already Ntiamoah was beginning to take her for granted. Seku knew that his friend drank a lot and liked women exceedingly, but he really thought a month was a very short period for him to be able to hold other women with the same lust he had for his wives.

'Not all men have the same beliefs as you do,' Ntiamoah was saying. 'I have three wives, Seku, all with hot thighs. You may not believe it, but I tell you it is so: the more women one has, the more women one wants. Sometimes I think it is a sickness. Maybe it is all these wars and killings one has to do, but I need a woman's company badly, yet after I have married her, our relationship becomes more one of brother and sister, and my lust is for women from without my house.'

Seku shrugged and smiled to show that it was not important. 'Yaw,' he changed the subject, 'I do not know all the people at your feast.'

Ntiamoah turned to cast a glance around, but shrugged carelessly. 'They are all drunk. We started in the afternoon, and you are only coming at sunset. You can meet them tomorrow, if you like, when they are sober.' He now turned back to the subject Seku had tried to change. 'I admire you, Seku, for reserving your manhood for only one hole. Of course, Mbinge is the most beautiful woman I have ever cast eyes upon – believe me, I have seen women – and if you weren't my best friend, I would surely find ways of entering her. Sometimes, I think, she has a hold on you, but I can never figure out what it is. Don't Asante women attract you? I know of many beautiful ones who would love to enjoy you, and some of them are from the most important houses in Kumasi, sometimes even the favourite wives of chiefs!'

'You flatter me, brother,' Seku laughed, 'but I know how much you exaggerate.' As Ntiamoah made as if to protest, he said, 'Look, they are dancing a new thing I have never seen before.'

So they watched the dancers. This time somebody was playing the part of an antelope being hunted by a man and two dogs. The dogs cornered the antelope, and then the hunter made his appearance with his bow. Seku was so impressed by the death-dance that he clapped very loudly, and the neighbouring drunken men also joined in, though they hadn't watched at all, but had concentrated on squeezing the soft bodies of the many cheap girls Ntiamoah had paid to entertain his guests.

Ntiamoah said, 'Everybody seems happy you are being honoured. Because you were so long in coming, I proposed a libation to your well-being before the people drank too much, and they seemed very happy and proud of you. Now some of them call you Osei Seku, Seku the destroyer.'

Seku laughed, somewhat embarrassed, 'I am flattered.'

'It is good,' Ntiamoah said with some mockery. 'Humility is a quality one should never lose.' He refilled Seku's calabash, and then a thought seemed to strike him, 'My brother! You must forgive me; I have been drinking too much. How is Mbinge the fair? How is the stomach?'

'It is well,' Seku took a sip. 'It shouldn't be long now, and I shall have perhaps a son, or maybe a daughter. It will be a very nice surprise for a man coming home from war to see that his actions before he left have been finally rewarded.'

'But your wife, I could never understand why she never gave birth. Naturally, I assumed you did your marital work regularly.'

Seku laughed, then replied in a more serious voice, 'We should have several children now. But as I have told you already my wife and I made a long journey from Mossi through Mamprusi and Dagomba to Asante.

It was very hard for her, and she had a miscarriage on the way. It was only when we reached Salaga, an important Dagomba trading town, that I could send her to a fetish priest to be examined. It cost me all I had, and we had to enter Kumasi absolutely penniless – just as when you met us. For a while I thought the priest had told lies with his cures, but now it has happened, and soon I shall hold my first child in my arms.'

'I am happy for you, Seku. But what name will you give the child?'

'If it's a girl, I am still not sure, but if it is a boy, he shall be named after my brother.'

'Your brother is dead?'

'Yes.'

'Your only brother?'

'From my mother, yes.'

'You have never told me of his death, brother Seku.'

'You have never asked.'

'I am asking now.'

'It is not important how it happened. Another time.'

'As you wish.' Ntiamoah took a sip and pinched a girl's waist before he said, 'A picture comes before my eyes of your great attack, the rout of the Gyaaman. I followed you closely, because I wanted to be at your side. I saw that it was not the commander of Gyaaman you wanted, but another fellow to his right. You missed a good opportunity to capture the general personally, but took after an apparently unimportant person as he made off. Am I talking the truth?'

Seku did not answer directly. 'Nevertheless,' he replied, 'the Asante generals are convinced it was my attack which saved the day.'

'But I am no general,' Ntiamoah answered. 'It does not interest me now that it was you who saved my balls that day, what I remember is that, at a moment when the fighting was to close that the guns were useless and we were outnumbered, you suddenly led a brilliant attack, but left the main prize, the commander-in-chief of Gyaaman, and took off after one man. I followed you, but arrived just as you were running him through. Who was he? I considered his attire as I came to your side, and decided he was no Gyaaman.'

Seku was silent for a long while. Then he turned to Ntiamoah, 'He was my country-man. He was in Mossi with me, and he was present when my brother was murdered. I killed him because he showed no regret, and said I would soon meet my end.'

'It is the woman?'

Now Seku was standing up, 'Yaw my brother, you are the man alive closest to my heart today. I do not intend to keep any secrets between us, but this story is a hard one for me. It is something I would rather forget. Today is your feasting day, a time for us all to be merry – not only you, but we your guests as well. Come, let us join the dancers.'

Ntiamoah made his apologies quickly, but Seku was already pulling at him. They stepped onto the courtyard, and the dancers made way and some of them even formed a dancing circle round them shouting and waving their white handkerchiefs in the air. Ntiamoah grabbed one girl and shouted over the music for Seku to do the same. He didn't have to grab; two girls voluntarily stepped forward, and he danced with both. They were much more accomplished dancers than he, and he found it difficult to keep up with their feet movements and swinging hips. As soon as he could he made his excuses and went to sit down again, leaving Ntiamoah on the floor. Now all dancers had stopped to give honour to the host, and were cheering him on gaily. Despite the alcohol in his stomach, Ntiamoah was very graceful, and could match the girl's dancing very well. Everybody was clapping merrily except for two figures standing directly opposite Seku across the courtyard. He thought they looked rather annoyed, and he recognised them as Antwiwaa and Mansa, his friend's first two wives. He couldn't make out where Amina was, and guessed she was somewhere in the kitchen.

Several hours later, he told Ntiamoah he had to be going, Ntiamoah stared at him. 'But you can't leave now. I've prepared a place for you.'

Seku thanked him, but said he had promised his wife to be home before midnight.

Ntiamoah shook his head sadly. 'You and your wife,' he said. 'There are numerous beautiful virgins here to enjoy, but you must go home to your wife to keep her company. What will you do? Her belly is swollen, and the most you can do is hold hands for hours on end. Or is there a maid at home who receives the mistress' dues for her?'

Seku laughed and pounded his back. Only one of his bodyguards came up to them at the main doorway. When Seku asked where the other was, he looked down and shuffled his feet in embarrassment.

Ntiamoah laughed and said, 'I think I know where he is.'

He went and pounded at a door, and the man hurried out, tying his cotton trousers into place, and he made his apologies to Seku.

Ntiamoah saw them off only a short distance, and said he had to return to show the guests the sleeping places. 'Else one may end up in my new wife's bed,' he explained seriously.

15

2

The outbreak of civil war in Asante came as a big blow of surprise for most Asante people. Osei Kwame was an unpopular king, and everybody knew he was increasingly disliked by the Amanhene, the other chiefs of the confederation of Asante states of which he was head. The year's Odwira Cleansing Festival in Kumasi ended in hot arguments between him and his chiefs, and everybody heaved a sigh of relief when the meeting broke up after many days of discussions, thinking it was over. But it was only the beginning of a more serious rift. The chiefs were tired of Osei's cruelty and strange ways, and they feared that he would embrace the Moslem religion and enforce it in all Asante. Not only did the Asante have their own religion of ancestor worship of which they were fiercely proud, but also they knew too little of Islam and were convinced that Osei Kwame would use it to enhance his own powers. Already Osei's relations with Moslems had reached such a stage that he preferred their advice to those of his constitutional chiefs. To forestall whatever plans he might have in his head they plotted to destool him.

Kumasi became the centre of a new wave of events. Osei Kwame heard of their plottings and fled to his kinsman, the chief of Dwabwen, the only one of his Amanhene on his side. The other chiefs made several attempts to bring him back to answer destoolment charges, but he paid no heed. At last they destooled him in absentia and a new ruler, Opoku II, was installed.

The Amanhene returned to their provinces, pleased with their work. But a great surprise was in store for the new king. Asante's thrust to the northern plains had incorporated large Moslem areas in the empire. Dagomba and Gonja were ruled by Moslem kings, and states like Gyaaman, though ruled by pagan chiefs, were Moslem in large areas. None of these rulers were consulted before the King was deposed, and they greatly resented the act. They were not concerned with his cruelties and short-comings at home: they saw that he gave respect to the Allah of Moslems. The people of Gyaaman sent envoys to the

Dyula of Kong, a powerful Moslem state to the north-west of Asante, and he offered assistance. They revolted and crossed the river Tano to invade Kumasi and to reinstate Osei Kwame as Asantehene.

During the war Kumasi became very dangerous. Osei Kwame still had his supporters in Kumasi, and with Asante concerned with the danger from the north they took great care to make life unpleasant for those who had stayed behind. There were frequent cases of persons disappearing from their homes, theft occurred on a scale unknown before, and several houses were burnt down at night while their occupants lay sleeping.

Punishment became severe for even the mildest crimes. The hated abrafo state executioners and the warriors of the Ankobea regiment* were given instructions to mete out immediate punishment to all criminals instead of arresting them for trial. There were reports that the younger abrafo took advantage of the opportunity to improve their head-cutting abilities. After being arrested an armed criminal would have his arms and feet tied, but in such a way that he could still walk, but slowly. One of the abrafo would then sever his head in a single stroke, and they made bets to see whose headless victim would take the most number of steps before collapsing.

But the abrafo were not the only cruel ones. One day Jakpa was awakened by a loud commotion coming from the harem buildings near his sleeping quarters in the palace. He hesitated about entering till some abrafo ran past him, then he followed. The eunuchs had arrested a sex-starved man who had actually dared to break into the harem and had undressed one of the King's young wives with obvious intentions. The fat leader of the eunuchs refused to turn over the rapist to the abrafo, saying that they had their own methods. They led the man outside, stripped him naked and sat him down on his buttocks. Three eunuchs held him still: a fourth lay a slab of rock under his testicles and squashed them flat with a single blow from another rock. Then they set the man free.

Jakpa and Maalam Fuseini were the only Moslems who still remained in the palace during the entire war. They were the only ones who had been secretly against Osei Kwame because of his cruelty and lack of wisdom.

News was not easy to obtain of the struggle occurring between the Asante and Gyaaman armies. Jakpa and Maalam Fuseini checked the records and made new ones of events happening and of decisions and

* The Ankobea regiment's duty was to guard Kumasi during wartime.

agreements reached in the Palace, but they were careful to remain neutral and to give no comment on how they really felt. Maalam Fuseini had been given some farming land by the former king, and if there was something they wanted to discuss, they went there and spoke Arabic so that unseen eavesdroppers could not understand.

At last messengers came with the news that the revolt had been defeated and Kumasi was full of the names of new heroes, the generals and leading warriors, the linguists who had controlled the policy concerning the accepted terms of the outcome. Maalam Fuseini was summoned by the king, and he returned to tell Jakpa that there would be work to do as soon as the leading officers of the campaign returned to give a report to the king.

'I am happy,' he said, 'that the new king still entrusts us to help in the documentation of events. After all these problems with Moslems, I frankly expected worse.'

A week later they were given the full details of the campaign and told to mention the places of the two main battles, the leading generals and linguists in the report. The king of Gyaaman had been deposed by the Asante army, and a new king, Adinkra, enstooled. Over five thousand of the more influential Moslems of Gyaaman had been arrested and were awaiting trial. One of the linguists asked them to mention the great role played by the Kambonse in the campaign. The Kambonse was a special detachment of the Asante army, being formed mainly of skilled musqueteers from Dagomba, but with a number of Gonja or Daboya men. The generals reported that at one point the Asante army was heavily pushed back and they feared defeat, but the Kambonse showed great courage, and led by one young Gonja, they forced an opening in the enemy ranks, and were the main reason for the rout of the Gyaaman.

The linguist added, 'Some important activities will take place in the town which you will be expected to record. First, there will be a funeral for all those who died for Asante, then soon after, the king will hold a grand durbar to honour those noblest warriors of the campaign. They will include the young man from Gonja, and I shall expect you to give special mention to him. We are increasingly becoming aware of the need to continue in the footsteps of Osei Tutu or Osei Kwadwo, and to achieve as much harmony as possible in Asante.'

Maalam Fuseini had been 30 years in the palace. A thin, frail man with a bald head, he nonetheless possessed a forceful drive that always impressed Jakpa. He had served ten years with Osei Kwadwo, who was succeeded upon his death by Osei Kwame, one of the most controversial of Asante's five kings since the Union was forged by Osei Tutu and his fetish priest Okomfo Anokye. When Osei Kwame was elected king, his mother chose to rule in his place till he came of age, thus breaking custom, as the chief of Mampong was by constitution the one who was second in rank in the whole land. After two years of disturbances in all Asante, the lady finally stepped down for her son, who soon started flirting with Mohammedanism, contrary to his advisor's pleas to avoid the strange religion. This fact won many Moslems to his side: soon Kumasi's Moslem populace had tripled to about eight thousand. About twenty of the most senior Moslems frequented his palace, though only four or five were actually needed to record events for the illiterate rulers of Asante.

At first Maalam Fuseini had been one of his favourites, but he slowly drew himself away from the king as he got to know him better. Osei Kwame was a heartless tyrant. He caused his own mother to be driven out of the palace because she warned him against his strong headedness, and he unnecessarily caused large numbers of victims to be sacrificed at certain festivals. What had caused the chiefs to hate him most was when it was discovered that he had caused the murder of his younger brother and heir-apparent Osei Poku who was very popular with the people, as well as that of Poku Amankwaa, one of the most handsome and likeable princes in Kumasi. To cover his crime the king had ordered over 1,500 people to be sacrificed to the shades of the murdered princes.

Maalam Fuseini had long expected the chiefs to rise against the king. He knew only too well that the king of Asante enjoyed no absolute power: his Amanhene could veto his decisions. But most of the other Moslems in Kumasi did not heed his advice. They wanted to exploit their unexpected champion to the full. They even showed their pleasure openly when the king followed their advice against his Asante advisors in minor affairs.

Mumula was one of the most influential Imams of the Palace. He was a tall, very black Dagomba, and he walked everywhere with the giant Bawa twins, the elder one of whom had recently been crowned Kokoa wrestling champion of all Kumasi. Mumula had been Maalam Fuseini's guest when he first arrived in Kumasi fifteen years before: now they were bitter enemies. Maalam Fuseini understood the man's disappointment. What Mumula and his friends wanted was to convert Osei Kwame to Islam, in the hope that he in turn would be lenient to the Moslem subject states of the plains which supplied most of Asante's slaves. They called him traitor because he had pointed out that the king would never allow himself to be converted as he was too bloodthirsty by nature: they wouldn't believe him when he said he would soon be deposed by his angry Amanhene.

When Osei Kwame got into serious debates with his chiefs, the quarrel of the Moslems of Kumasi flared into hot accusations that Maalam Fuseini and his friends were influencing the chiefs – which was quite untrue. Tula, his assistant for five years, was murdered in a thicket when he was coming to give a report on his writing. Two days later Maalam Fatai, his closest friend for twenty years, and the only senior Imam in Kumasi openly on his side, was axed at the doorstep of his house.

Maalam Fuseini was lucky to come across Jakpa a few months before the outbreak of War. With his two most trusted companions dead, he feared for his life and asked the Gyaasehene, Finance Minister of Asante and his friend for many years, for four guards. When the Gyaasehene told him that one of his friends had a slave who could read and write he had been sure it was a near-illiterate whom he would have to teach for years before he would be of any use to him. To his surprise he found that Jakpa was indeed a great scholar who could even surprise him at times by quoting passages of the Koran he had not mastered himself. He had thanked Allah for His gift in his darkest moment, and afraid that Jakpa might be murdered like Tula, he asked the Gyaasehene to accommodate him in the palace. This building was in reality a huge collection of houses and courtyards, the largest courtyard being about 80 yards by 300, in which people might gather at certain occasions. Numerous servants, guards and officials had their rooms there. Jakpa's own courtyard was among those of the palace eunuchs who served in the large harem nearby.

Now the war was over at last. The Moslems of Kumasi looked at him with awe and fear, for he had been prôved right. But the Imam did not feel joy at having won the argument: he was only relieved that the whole affair was over, and he hoped that his former enemies would soon become his friends. He was also a man of the northern plains: his people were suffering as much as, if not more than any others, from slavery. He was glad Osei Kwame the cruel had been deposed, but he was not happy that the people of Asante would still go on selling others to the White men of the Great Sea.

*　　*　　*

Jakpa was a young man of twenty-four, but experience had made an older man out of him. For nearly two years he was a slave, first in Dagomba, where he was captured, and later in Kumasi. His Kumasi master, Nana Amoaten, had been an envoy of the king. He went at the scheduled times to collect the contribution of slaves from Dagomba to Asante. When he was bringing down his slaves he had appeared harsh and cruel to Jakpa, but as he got to know him better he saw that the man was actually kind-hearted at home. He had two secrets which Jakpa found out whilst serving him. First, he could no longer have children. He had lost the power during a slave rebellion about four years before he met Jakpa, and so he greatly spoilt those three children his two wives had given him before the incident. They said that a slave striving to escape had blown himself up with a stolen barrel of gunpowder when he was surrounded by the guards. A rock uplifted by the explosion landed on Amoaten's groin, and caused his sickness. His second secret was his ambitions concerning his pretty niece, Akosua Kyem. According to Asante tradition inheritance was matrilineal, and as Akosua's mother was dead, it meant Akosua was the custodian of his family tree. He was determined that no commoner should pollute the blood of his ancestral tree, and he wanted a marriage with no less a person than a senior official from the king's palace itself.

For nine long months Jakpa had toiled in their household, tilling the man's farm, weeding the area round the house and outdoor toilet to discourage snakes from coming too close, building or repairing storage barns. He had a piece of white cloth in which he wrote the simple words 'Salaam Aleikum', and when Amoaten discovered the cloth he hurried to Kumasi and 'donated' Jakpa to the palace, for which the Gyaasehene gave him a rich compensation for his loss.

Ever since his freedom, he occasionally went to visit Amoaten to show his respects. He hadn't been for a long time now since the war ended, and he decided to go with his servant Kofi to the market to speak with Akosua and Maame Ntosuor, the oldest slave in Amoaten's house, who was present when the man was born.

They were pleased to see him. He sat in the shade of their stall and watched them selling their fresh foodstuffs – cocoyam, plantain, cassava, yam, vegetables and fruits. Most of the buyers brought other goods to barter with – cloths, sandals, eggs and even one black piglet. This was quite normal in Asante at that time. Only the upper classes could afford to buy their goods with the specially shaped brass pieces recognised as money by law: occasionally the wives of well-to-do elders even purchased their items with gold dust.

They cooked in the market, yam and nkontomire sauce, but Jakpa had to turn down their invitation, as the Ramadan was not yet over.

They all nodded in understanding except Akosua, who remarked loudly, 'Ei, now our friend the Kramo eats only the best of food, and even then, only with his equals.'

Jakpa was embarrassed, but Maame Ntosuor came to his rescue saying, 'Don't mind her, Jakpa. She is spoilt, and can't get used to the idea that you are now an important man who has to be treated with respect.'

Jakpa asked about Nana Amoaten's health. Only a few weeks before, he had lost his job of bringing down slaves from the north, because the new king had shuffled the various posts in order to give rewarding responsibilities to his many supporters. Amoaten had remained neutral during the quarrel between the two kings, so he was nicely invited to the palace, given many presents and then quietly dismissed. Now the one-time official had to depend solely on his farm, and the last time Jakpa had seen him he had been bitter and unhappy.

Maame Ntosuor replied that he would soon get over his disappointment. She said that he would soon realise that being a farmer was more decent than to be a transporter of human beings for use as beasts by Asante. Jakpa had always respected her for her boldness, and he knew that although she was Amoaten's property, even he respected and feared her too. Jakpa and all the other inhabitants of the household called her 'Nana,' Grandparent, the superlative title of respect, and the older Amoaten and his wives addressed her as 'Maame' – Mother.

When it was time for him to go Akosua offered a large bunch of plaintain. 'Please take it. We have brought too much to the market, and it would be nice not to have to carry it all back.'

He thanked her, but said it was much too bulky and besides, he didn't like her to make a loss.

She was more friendly now. 'Kofi can carry it,' she nodded at his personal servant. 'And as for the loss, I already owe you some plantain. Don't you remember? On the day you left for the palace I promised to send you plantain, but I never did. Well, here it is.'

So he helped Kofi load the huge bunch onto his head. The poor man flinched with discomfort, and Akosua said, 'You forgot the kashire.'

The 'kashire' was a soft thick folding of old cloth placed on the head before the load was in place, so that it served to cushion the weight. This time they both helped Kofi to load, and she said, rather secretively, 'You aren't angry with me, are you, Jakpa?'

He assured her he was not.

'But you have hardly spoken with anybody else but Nana. Don't you like my conversation?'

He assured her he did. 'But I must go now to the Imam. I promised to see him this afternoon.'

'Is it about the durbar the Asantehene is holding?'

He nodded.

'Ah,' she said excitedly. 'There is a man from your country among their number. Do you know that?'

He smiled. 'Yes.'

'Have you met him yet?'

This time he laughed. 'No, Akosua. I can't even imagine what he is like, nor can I guess which part of Gonja exactly he comes from. You see, he is being honoured as a member of the Kambonse, a branch of the Asante army. As you may know already, all members of the Kambonse have Asante day-names. His is Kwame, implying that he first joined on a Saturday. That is all I know so far, and it isn't much.'

She smiled mischievously. 'I know more than you do. Nana,' she turned to Maame Ntosuor, 'I know more than the Asantehene's secretary. He doesn't even know the man from his country who is being honoured.'

Jakpa asked, 'Do you know him?'

'Yes.'

'Is he another of your suitors?'

She did not seem to find that funny. 'No!'

'What is his name?'

'Guess.'

'Jakpa.'

'No, try again.'

'Jakpa the lesser.'

'No.'

'Please tell me. I give up.'

'Come and find out.'

'What?'

'I said come and find out.'

'I am sorry, Akosua, but the Imam —'

'But it's not far. Come, we shall go to his wife's stall. She fries bean-cakes in the market.' She turned to Maame Ntosuor, 'Nana, I am going to show him the place.'

Jakpa looked at Maama Ntosuor for help, but she said, 'Go with her, Jakpa. It is not far. I think you should make friends with them. Not only is he your countryman, but he is also very influential in Kumasi, and could be useful. His wife is a kind woman, and if she sees you, she will surely arrange for you to meet him. It is well known that she has great influence on him.'

So they went off to look for the woman, Kofi following with his load. Now Jakpa had a good opportunity to realise really how big the market was. In all his visits he had only come to Akosua's stall, which was not far from one of the many entrances. There were numerous narrow roads on either sides of which were wares spread out for sale.

Many people had stalls and tables to show off their goods, some had only tables and the very poor had old cloths spread on the ground, and there they had arranged their wares: foodstuffs, smoked fish and meat, hides, knives, cutlasses, cooking pots, sandals, cloth, various forms of alcohol – palm wine, pito, akpeteshie. Most of the sellers were women. They generally wore the same sort of kaba and cloth as Akosua had, with huge broad-rimmed straw hats as a protection against the hot sun. Some were exceedingly fat – they were often the richest and most influential market mammies, and it was said that they used their wealth to seduce handsome young men.

'I am surprised you haven't heard of her,' Akosua said as they turned their second bend. 'She is very beautiful, and I am sure men discuss her a lot.'

He replied that Maalam Fuseini was not exactly the kind of man to discuss women, and they both laughed.

'She is a lucky woman. Not only is she beautiful, but she has a good husband. He is a man different from all others. He keeps only one wife, despite the fact that many women in this town are after him. He ignores all attempts to seduce him. Jakpa, you asked a while ago if he was my suitor. To tell you the truth, if such a man wanted me, I would elope with him if necessary, breaking my uncle's heart. I think it is just not fair how women are cheated by men.'

'So, so,' he said teasingly. 'That is why you make friends with him, eh? What has happened to your other suitors?'

She could not answer because just then two muscular sweating men passed them, going in the opposite direction, and they had to step aside. Both were carrying heavy sacks of charcoal, and it was obvious from their approach that they would not give way. The second one spat carelessly, and Jakpa jumped to avoid being touched by the slimy fluid.

24

He was very annoyed and wanted to run after the fellow, but Akosua laughed and pulled at his smock.

'Come, Kramo. You are in a hurry, remember? This happens everyday in the market. One just has to be careful.'

So they carried on, and his anger died down.

Now he was beginning to wonder how many people were in the market: all roadways seemed full of people, though it was already noon, and they could advance only slowly. How many people were there in Kumasi? Thousands and thousands, and if one considered the neighbouring villages, perhaps four times as many in all. He remembered that one of the linguists had said that Kumasi had over a hundred thousand people, but the Imam had later said he thought it was around fifty thousand, and perhaps about two hundred thousand when one also counted all the surrounding villages. The Asante never bothered to count their subjects, but the Imam had lived three years in Dahomey, where the Fon insisted upon regularly counting his people in all settlements, and so he should know. At the same instance Jakpa remembered that the only people ever to crush a complete Asante expedition since the time of Osei Tutu were the Dahomeans, assisted by the Oba of Oyo. It was the reign of Kusi Obodom when the Akyem rebelled against Asante rule assisted by the Fon of Dahomey. Asante troops quickly overran Akyem and won it back, and the king sent a large expedition to teach the Dahomeans a lesson. The Asante defeat was complete, and the elders were so disgusted that they destooled the old, nearly blind monarch and installed Osei Kwadwo on the Golden Stool. From what the Imam had told him, Jakpa understood Dahomey to be a state organised purely for war, with regiments of women.

He stopped. 'It seems too far away, Akosua. Can't we go another time?'

'But we are almost there. Just round the next bend, and —'

But they turned twice before she pointed ahead towards an open-sided stall. The woman was selling a customer some of her cakes, and had her back to them. There was a vague familiarity about the bottom, but Jakpa could not place her immediately. Somehow the Asante cloths seemed odd on her. Now she turned to stir the frying pan, and he saw her belly was swollen out of proportion. She lifted her head to swat at a fly, and at last her face was revealed as the broad-rimmed hat moved up and out of the way.

'Isn't she beautiful? I wish God had given me just a fraction of her looks: the fingers, the lips – Jakpa, what is the matter?'

He had stopped. His mouth was open as if he could not believe his eyes, and the initial surprise changed slowly into a look of sad pain even as she watched.

'Are you not coming? Jakpa, what is wrong?'

He did not seem to hear. He took her hand and led a hasty retreat, looking back for a last time before they turned round a stall stacked high with charcoal.

'Jakpa, I do not understand. Why are you going?'

He ignored her question and asked, 'How long have you known her?'

She replied stubbornly, 'You haven't answered my question.' But the look on Jakpa's face was something new for her. She had always imagined him to be soft-willed and weak, but now his face frightened her, and she saw that she had never really understood his ways during his nine months at her home. The obedient slave, then the respectful Kramo, with a face of outer calm which could be a useful tool to keep hidden his most inner secrets. It suddenly came to her how little she really knew of him. Of his life before Kumasi she only knew that he was a Gonja who had been captured by the Dagomba in order to be sent to Kumasi to help meet the slave-quota. She had no idea what sort of life he had led while living in his own land. She answered, 'I have known her for about two months. We met in the market, and we have exchanged many visits, especially when her husband was at war.'

'Where do they live?'

'Aboabo, a quarter of the town. They have a big home there with many servants.'

'And where is her husband?'

'I don't know. Perhaps at home, or with one of his friends.'

'They have many children?'

'No, she is expecting for the first time.'

He nodded silently.

She said, 'Jakpa, she is a good woman. She never did anybody harm.'

'Do you think I want to harm her?

She did not answer.

'What makes you think that way?'

'You know her, don't you?'

'Have you told her of me?'

'Yes, but only in passing.'

'Did she show great surprise or fear?'

'No.'

'Then why should I harm her?'

26

'I don't know.'

'What did she say when you told her about me?'

'She seemed surprised at first, then she said she would tell her husband. She said that it would be nice for him to make friends with his countryman.'

'I see.'

'Jakpa,' she asked quietly, 'who are you?'

'What do you ask? I am Jakpa, the same one as always.'

'No – I mean, you know her, but she doesn't know you. Why is it so?'

He laughed. 'She is beautiful, as you yourself have said. Must I be blamed for admiring her?'

'You are hiding something from me. You knew her before Kumasi, didn't you?'

'Who knows? The world is a big place.'

'Were you a suitor?'

He laughed again, the same loud but mirthless cackle.

'No. Do I look rich enough to court such beauties? I entered Kumasi a slave, and if it weren't for your uncle and the Imam, I wouldn't have a cloth round my hips today.'

'It is said that those who read and write are never slaves in the north.'

'Perhaps I was an exception.'

She looked doubtfully at him. But Jakpa had had enough of the discussion, and he reminded her that he had to meet Maalam Fuseini. She accompanied him to the nearest exit from the market. Then as he said goodbye she said, 'I shall keep your secret, Jakpa.'

He stared at her, started to say something, then thought better of it. He bowed slightly and walked away, taking long strides so that the short Kofi struggled in his wake in a half-walk, half-run, staggering under the weight of the huge bunch of plantain.

3

The elders of Kumasi had decided to reward Seku with a large plot of farm land far away in the Sefwi forests. A junior linguist from the palace was entrusted to take him to inspect his new property.

Mbinge dressed very carefully to wish her husband goodbye, though he was expected to be away for little more than a week. Seku was sorry she couldn't come along too, but he knew her time would soon come. She looked so beautiful that he boasted to himself mentally, 'Not even the king has a woman like this!'

As they walked away Seku's mind soon left his wife, and he thought more of the wealth and prestige soon to be his. He hardly knew then that those few moments of the morning would constitute some of the most important memories of his later life.

They needed four days to reach their destination. The farms lay in the Sefwi forest to the west of Kumasi. In the first two days they slept in two villages, but on the third they had already reached the thickest jungle in all Asante, so they made camp under the trees and lit fires in four corners as a protection against snakes.

It was indeed an adventure for Seku. They were led by guides through great expands of marshy land in the forest. Occasionally they surprised a few animals: the rodents scampered off quickly, but the snakes seemed to be lords of the jungle and only went slowly, unhurriedly away. Once they came across a black cobra eating a dead cutting grass. Since snakes have no cutting teeth, and the rodent was much too large for the cobra to swallow, the meat had to be foul and soft before it could tear off chunks to swallow. It was lying right across the path and paid no heed as they stood watching. Seku drew his sword, but the linguist laughed.

'Let him be, my lord,' he said. 'The beasts of the forest have no hate for man. They kill only to eat and only strike when in danger.' To prove his point he pushed the meat a little away from the deadly serpent. It slithered after its meal, still showing no awareness of the presence of the men. One by one they stepped over it and continued on their way.

At another time one of the guides held Seku back and pointed. Seku only saw the lianas; the man swung his stick and a long green snake was knocked down, but it recovered quickly and escaped into the bushes.

The linguist told Seku, 'That was the mamba. Its bite is more dangerous than any other snake's because it aims for the chest and upwards, and not the lower leg. The gods were with you.'

Seku hated and feared the thick gloom in which only few birds sang. Even the sun hardly penetrated the dense roof of leaves. He hoped that it would not be necessary for him to visit the place again after this occasion.

He was relieved when at last they came to the settlement in the forest where many of the king's newest officials were given farming land. Seku liked the headman, who was a very simple and honest-looking man. They held a little drumming festival in his honour and when he went to bed they sent a slave-girl along to 'warm his bed'. It was no new thing for Seku – he always sent the girls to sleep in a corner. In the past year he had been offered at least twelve such nights, but never had he broken his vow to Mbinge.

The next day they showed him his lands: half of it had obvious signs of previous farming – he was told it used to belong to an Asante general who had stubbornly supported Osei Kwame, and had lost his property with Osei's destoolment. The other half across a stream was still thick jungle.

In the evening they held an even bigger durbar for him, and Seku really enjoyed himself. The linguist had told him that all inhabitants of the forest, including the headman, were slaves. Now Seku asked himself, how is it that of all people the most cheerful are the oppressed? They had the merriest laughter, the best jokes and were the best musicians of all. The chiefs and noblemen of Kumasi had wealth and power – they could flog servants and slaves to within a tiny stop from death with impunity. In the case of an important chief it was even authorised by law and custom that his favourite slaves should accompany him to the land of the dead. These men condemned to live many years, perhaps their whole lives, in the midst of nowhere toiling to increase the wealth of war-lords enjoying royal support, could they rebel? No, of course not, the Asante Army would crush any such attempt. Yet the great wonder was that the lords of Kumasi wore troubled faces as they counted the days for their enjoyment of royal favour, whereas those who had nothing of material wealth and were often as lowly in Asante as mere beasts had the finest laughter and the best cheer. It was a strange thing indeed.

Seku's mind went back to his years in Mossi. There had been numerous slaves in the village, but they had been mostly poor peasants who offered their services to nobles in return for shelter and protection, and it was not abnormal for the more intelligent ones to win their freedom in some way or other, and rise on to become important men with their own servants and slaves.

Seku thought of his father, and he felt some stirrings of shame. He had been a great learned Imam, and an outspoken opponent of Asante and her slaving methods. Seku had been one of his favourite sons, but he had disappointed the old man by his lack of interest for Arabic. Sometimes the Imam lost his temper, and chained Seku for hours to a stake away from any tree that might give shade from the hot sun. One day Seku rebelled. After one such chaining, when the Imam sent servants to free him, he left the village for two days, keeping away from any areas of human settlement. When he finally returned he went boldly to his anxious father and told him that he wanted to stop learning Arabic.

The old man was very apprehensive. He pleaded with his son to forgive him his rashness in wanting to push him to greatness 'within a day'. He reminded him that he had been record-keeper in the Gonja court before coming to Mossi, and that the post was passed on preferably from father to son.

Seku felt his temper rising: he could barely keep the anger out of his voice: 'Baba, you tell us to believe in something that isn't there anymore. Gonja is no more – it is overrun with Asante warriors, and you tell us this yourself that you barely managed to escape alive. You tell us of Allah the just, but Allah allowed the Berber hoards to storm Timbuctu, burning all books and looting Mali of its treasures. Allah allowed the infidel Asante to enter our city to enslave our people. I do not believe in Allah, Baba. He is a myth. The gods of Mossi and Asante are surely more powerful, because they protect their worshippers.'

The Imam knelt slowly on his goat skin. He picked up the beads, and asked Seku to leave him alone to pray.

After this event Seku had given up Arabic completely, and his father had made no protest even when he did not pray anymore, and worse, when he started seeing Mossi fetishes for cures when he got ill. The Imam had not cursed his son; he had even made up with him in all ways except in religion, but even here he had never complained, but had seemed reconciled to his fate. He had died long before Seku had left Mossi, and there had been no strains or shame for Seku, who knew that only his father's strong love had prevented him from cursing his son for thus disappointing him. He hoped that he had found his peace finally with his Allah.

Seku's relationship with Moslems had worsened even more since his quarrel with the Moslem Fulani over the death of Suley, whom he had beaten in the Kokoa. He avoided Moslems, because though he had broken away from them, there was still some fascination he felt for them, and he knew and hated the fact that as far as Moslems were concerned, all non-believers were 'unclean'. The only Moslem he had respected in Kumasi was Maalam Fatai, who had sheltered him and Mbinge when the Fulani were out for his blood. Seku had been far from Kumasi in Praso when he heard the news of his death, and he had cried like a child. He would have liked to return to mourn his death, but at that time he was only a very junior recruit at Prasu, so he had done the next best thing: he had visited the graveyard upon returning to Kumasi, and made a humble prayer there for the man.

Seku's father has been an outspoken critic of slavery. He had hated Asante for imposing this sickness on his land, and in Mossi he had never called any of his servants slaves: they were his 'children', and they all called him 'Baba', Father. Seku knew that he would be hurt about his son having joined the Asante army, that is, if the dead really observed the living. Seku had prayed aloud to him for a whole night in his room in Zongo upon telling Ntiamoah his decision, and he had explained his reasons: his insecurity with the Fulani in Kumasi, and above all, his wish to give his wife a respectable home. She had borne all hardships with him without complaint, but Seku had got tired of feeling ashamed that he should have taken her from her home to offer only a beggar's life. He knew that Mbinge herself disagreed with his joining the Asante army, but she had complained only on the first night he had told her, and since then they had never mentioned the topic. Seku smiled dreamily as he remembered her, and he made it a point to ask Konadu the next day to help him choose the most worthy present for a pregnant wife waiting for her beloved husband's return.

When the party broke up for everybody to return home, a girl was sent to Seku to entertain him in bed. For the first time ever, he nearly broke his vow. As usual he first sent her to a corner of the room, but no sooner was he lying down than he felt some pleasant sensations around his groin. His feeling hands touched those of the girl. She had crawled forward in the darkness and very softly slipped her arms under the sleeping cloth. As if from far away Seku felt some throbs of shame in his head: his conscience told him to send her away. But for the better part of a year his manhood had done no useful work, and now it was stiff and trembling with desire. The girl's body was soft and tempting; when he placed a finger between her thighs it was wet. He wondered vaguely who she was because it was much too dark to see her face. Perhaps one of the female dancers from the hamlet, but it really didn't matter now. She let her body sag down beside him, and she helped him to a position above her parted legs. Seku's long fast which had weakened his self-discipline now came to the rescue. Even as the thing touched her thigh, the thick liquid gushed out in spasms, and he collapsed beside her again, weak. The girl moved sideways so as not to lie in the generous flow of sticky fluid, and she waited for him to recover his strength. But Seku said quietly, 'Let me be, girl. If you try again, I shall enter you with this,' and he let her feel the sharp end of his dagger.

That night Seku had a terrible dream. He woke up in the darkness, sweating profusely. He could only remember the last part of the dream, and it filled him with fear. There was he himself, running with a distended penis after a hen, and Mbinge was chasing after him and calling his name piteously, but he wouldn't pay heed. At last he caught up with the hen, then he was suddenly a cock mounting her. Enraged, Mbinge took a sharp knife and beheaded both hen and cock, but the cock's head rolled away and turned back into Seku's head. She didn't notice this; she prepared a fire on the spot and cooked the chickens after plucking and cleaning the flesh. She didn't eat, however, but seemed to be waiting. A man came up to her. He held a spear in one hand, and horror of horrors, there was no face – no eyes, ears or mouth but a tight piece of skin covering the front part of the head. Even more amazing was his wife's reaction – she had lowered her body to the ground, legs open facing the monstrosity, and on her face was a happy smile. The thing moved calmly up to her, then it thrust the spear into her and out again, once, twice, thrice. Seku's head was springing magically up and down with excitement, yet Mbinge was making the same sounds she made when he took her. The fourth thrust was so deep that half the spear disappeared into her, and Seku was suddenly awake.

He could see no sign of dawn through the small spaces between door and wall, and he wondered how many more hours he would have to wait before the sun rose. He had no idea at all how long he had slept. He reached out to touch the sleeping slave maid, and was relieved to find

32

her still there just beyond his feet on the straw mat, softly breathing. He settled back in bed, but his heart was pounding too heavily for sleep of any kind to come.

He said to himself, Seku, you are afraid. It is a dream of fate, and coward that you are, you can only jump up and down while a man smaller than yourself enters your woman with a spear. Shame on you, you whom the Asantehene himself is rewarding for bravery.

An owl hooted, unusually close, and he was gripped for a moment with the deepest terror. The scream was bursting in his head, but miraculously he managed to swallow it. Coward, he repeated, cowardly killer of poorly armed Gyaaman sons, be a man and look outside.

He got up and removed the wooden bars behind the door and walked into the courtyard. It was a moonless night – even the stars were few and dull in the heavens. The crickets and frogs supplied a steady humming music; occasionally an owl hooted or a dog far away barked. There was a light behind the gate of the compound home. He peeped through the space between the wall and the gate, and saw three men leaning on spears around a fire – the sentries, he guessed immediately.

He watched them for a long time, recovering his wits. But when he re-entered his room fear hit him again with terrific force, and he came out and stood peeping through the gates at the sentries, silently grateful for the sight of living people.

The thing, the thing. True there was no face, but the body belonged to only one person. Seku was saying to himself, there is no peace, there never shall be peace. Spirit of my lord – yes, for he is my lord – dear spirit, I did you wrong, but leave my wife alone even if it is because of her that I wronged you. I have had no peace of mind since that day, and were it not for her I should be mad now and I would long have committed suicide. I know that I must die, but I beg of you, let me reach such a position that even upon my death she shall not continue to suffer the poverty and hardship I have made her lot these many years, she who is a princess...

He stayed there till dawn, too afraid to go back to sleep. The girl was the first person of the house to get up. She called him softly, and he turned swiftly, his arms raised, with fear in his eyes. Seeing it was only her he shouted angrily, and she left him alone. He fetched himself water from the large barrels and pots in the compound, and had a bath.

He wanted to leave that very morning for Kumasi, so great was his fear. But the headman and linguist pleaded with him to stay one more day to speak with experts to advise him on the crops to choose for his farm. Their calmness made him feel ridiculous. He couldn't bring himself to discuss his dream with them, and he missed Ntiamoah greatly. But he agreed to stay a day longer in the farm.

Two days later they got the message from Kumasi. The Sefwi farms lay a day and a half behind them, and they were hoping to reach a village outside the Sefwi forest before nightfall. The bearers bore heavy loads: gifts from the headman and his subjects, and both Seku and the linguist had secured many presents for their friends and families. It had rained the night before: Seku had adjusted his cloth to halfway up his thighs to protect it from the mud. The linguist had found a simpler solution – he was astride the biggest bearer's shoulders, and he chattered endlessly, as if ignorant of the others' tiredness.

Suddenly one of the leading guards stopped. The others followed his example and listened too, but at first Seku heard nothing extraordinary: the frogs, cicadas and birds still sang on. Then he realised what it was. Some of the distant music ahead was abruptly cut off for several moments before it started again. Something – or someone – was approaching. The guards put a hand to their swords, but nobody actually drew the weapons out.

A slender man burst into view. It was a runner sent by Ntiamoah to tell Seku that a sad event had happened in his house in his absence. He told Seku that Mbinge had been stabbed by Siaka, Suley's brother, and that she lay in mortal danger.

Thus Seku's dream had indeed been a dream of fate, but he had allowed the headman and linguist to make him ignore its warning.

To his companions he looked like a man in a trance, so deep was the shock, and they felt wonder. But inside his mind was deadly calm. It was as if his inner emotions had been completely cut off and all energy concentrated for the task ahead.

He ran for Kumasi as no man had ever raced before. The messenger and a servant accompanied him, but he left them both far behind. He covered the remaining distance within 8 hours, whereas on the way to Sefwi they had needed nearly three days, or thirty-five hours of walking. This deed later earned him the nickname of 'Amirika', the Runner.

When Jakpa saw Seku's wife for the first time in the market, he thought for many days about what he had to do. Seku Wattara had wronged him, and whilst he was a slave he had sworn to kill him. With his freedom and subsequent elevation to court-secretary he had all but

34

forgotten about the couple, but now the painful memories came rushing back, and he hated Seku all the more for doing so well among the Asante.

He went to see the king's blacksmith and asked him to prepare him two daggers. Still, he hesitated about carrying out his plans.

He lost interest in everything else. He pretended pleasure when Maalam Fuseini told him about his having made peace with the other Moslems of Kumasi. The Imam had started a book on Asante with Jakpa's help; now he had to correct the young man's writings frequently, whereas a few weeks before he had believed that Jakpa was intellectually just as good as he. He told Jakpa that he planned to open a Moslem school in Kumasi with Jakpa and his erstwhile enemy Mumula as his assistants, but the young man's indifference showed through his polite words of thanks. Maalam Fuseini was hurt – what greater honour could one offer a Moslem Scholar than by giving him a chance to start a school? But he decided to be patient with his assistant, because after all, he had been faultless till only a few weeks ago; perhaps his love approaches had been rejected by some proud lady. Every young man, he thought sadly, had the right to undergo such an experience on the way to full manhood. He had become very fond of Jakpa, and would wait for him to recover.

Jakpa heard about Seku's journey to Sefwi, and for a while toyed with the idea of laying an ambush in the forest for him, but he had to reject the temptation because Seku would surely be with guards, whereas he would be alone.

He heard about Mbinge's incident when he went to visit Amoaten in his house. Both Akosua and Maame Ntosuor were away, and when he asked they told him that they were at Seku's house. Mbinge had been stabbed by Siaka, the Fulani whose younger brother Seku had killed in his only Kokoa wrestling match in Kumasi four years before.

Jakpa stayed in the palace, waiting for Seku's return. The incident had become popular with the abrafo executioners, so Jakpa regularly joined them in their conversations to hear if Seku had returned. But despite his hate for Seku he suffered each time they talked of his wife's pain.

About four days after Mbinge's stabbing Jakpa had an unexpected visit from Akosua. He opened the door of his room to find her waiting there. She had dressed up in bright colours, and had cooked some food for him. He was surprised at her boldness in coming to the palace, but she told him:

35

'Everybody knows you once lived in my household. It is quite normal for us to consider each other as brother and sister.'

He was embarrassed, and afraid that some of the palace workers would report the incident to her uncle. In Asante the penalty for seducing a virgin outside marriage was death, though the guilty one could 'buy his head' with a fine.

But he couldn't very well turn the girl away, so he ate her food and she watched him. He was uneasy, because he suspected that she had come to discuss her friend with him, and the last thing he wanted to discuss was Seku or his wife. To his surprise she burst into tears when he asked her what had brought her to him, and weepingly told him she was afraid that her uncle was going to marry her off to an old warrior called Nana Kuntunkuni.

Jakpa knew Kuntunkuni well. When Osei Kwame had ordered victims to be seized and sacrificed to the shades of the princes he had murdered, Jakpa had broken the curfew of respect in his ignorance and had been taken to the temple of sacrifice. But Kuntunkuni's son, an obrani by profession, had recognised him and taken him to his father's home. Amoaten had been this man's favourite assistant for ten years before he had taken over his job of transporting the slave quota from Dagomba to Kumasi. He sent Jakpa to Amoaten's home with greetings for his master the following morning.

Jakpa promised to speak to Nana Amoaten. He felt sorry for Akosua because he had always liked her, though he wasn't sure if he could in fact influence her uncle who wanted to marry her to wealth and security.

She thanked him, and asked if he had heard of Mbinge's accident. She explained that Maame Ntosuor was helping to nurse her, as she herself was afraid of deep wounds.

Jakpa had not wanted her to discuss this matter. But curiosity overcame him and he asked, 'Is it so bad? Will she survive?'

She said she didn't know, and he sat on his stool, suddenly melancholy

'Jakpa,' Akosua asked softly. 'Did you love her very much?'

He nodded slowly. 'But I never touched her. She was a sister and a hero both in one for me.'

'Then you must go and visit her, Jakpa. I know it may be a hard sight, but . . .' she stopped.

He shook the head. 'She doesn't know that I am here. She doesn't

36

even know I still live. Ill as she is, she will see me as a ghost, and it may be worse for her.'

She told him that Siaka had been arrested by the Abrafo, and was awaiting trial by the elders. He had laid an ambush for his enemy's wife at the outdoor pit latrine, and struck her in the upper part of the belly. The two maids of the house had come to see what the screams were all about, and had seen the man sprinting for the woods, and their mistress in a spreading pool of blood. They carried her inside and sent for help.

According to Maame Ntosuor, who was helping to nurse Mbinge, the wound was not very deep, but it had started to get gangrenous after a few hours. She did not appear to be in much pain, but the fetish priests and nurses were particularly worried if her birth pains would start before she could be out of real danger.

Jakpa listened in silence to her report. When she was through he said, 'Akosua.'

'Yes?' she looked at him.

'I want you to promise me this: stay with her.'

She looked surprised. 'Me? But I've told you that I fear deep wounds. Besides, what use would I be?'

He held her shoulders. 'Remember what you said this very evening? "We are like brother and sister." I want you to do for me what I daren't: serve her, and tell me regularly how her condition is.'

'Maame Ntosuor tells me everything.'

'I want you to do it for me. By all means go with Maame Ntosuor, but do go. Please promise.'

She seemed to be searching deep in his eyes for something, then she lowered her eyes and said, 'I shall do it, Jakpa.'

'I thank you, my sister.'

It was at this point that she saw the goatskin bag lying in the other room near his bed. He followed her gaze and she sensed his uneasiness.

'Where did you get that from?' she asked.

He tried to sound casual, but he knew he couldn't have convinced a deaf and blind man. 'A friend. Why do you ask? Has your uncle lost a similar design?'

She suddenly dashed past him into the bedroom. He reached out to stop her, but he only caught the knot of her under-cloth, and Akosua was immediately naked from the waist down but for a piece of small cloth around the genital parts, kept in place by a string of beads around the waist. While he stood gaping for an instant she ignored the incident and reached into the bag.

37

The blacksmith certainly knew his job. The two identical daggers had two-edged pointed blades as long as a man's lower forearm. The metal was highly polished and reflected light surprisingly well even in the dimmer light indoors. On the handle of each was the golden engraving of the Y-shaped Nyamedua, exactly as Jakpa had asked for.

Akosua said quietly, 'The king's blacksmith once forged an expensive sword for my uncle and sent the finished product in a similar bag.'

He made no reply.

'Tell me, Jakpa, why do you hate him so?'

He asked quickly, 'Who do you mean?'

'You know.'

He shrugged and looked away.

'Did he wrong your family? Was he a personal rival who got the woman you wanted?'

'Shut up!' he yelled aggressively.

'I shall not keep quiet, Jakpa,' she said calmly. 'Mbinge is my beloved friend, today she lies in mortal danger, you tell me you love her, you want me to help her, then you have daggers prepared for her beloved husband. Why?'

'I have told you she was never my lover,' he answered. 'Yes, I admired her and loved her as a sister and felt proud of her because of her beauty. I greatly respect her this very moment. She is a born princess, a pearl any man would be proud to call friend. For her I have the best of wishes, a happy life with all life's pleasures. But as for the man who abducted her from her land, he must die a most painful death!'

'Jakpa!' She was too shocked to weep or cry. She had never heard him use such hateful words. He had always been the soft gentle one, the one you felt you could trust for kindness at any moment. Never, whilst in her household, had he shown aggressiveness. Even when the abrafo had beaten and dragged him to and from the temple of sacrifice, he had still maintained the philosophical outlook of a man not to be broken in by threat of death. She had been ruder with him than with any of the other male servants, and even upon his summons to the palace she had often been cheeky to him without his losing his peaceful outlook. To hear him now talk of painful death was terrible.

He saw the doubts and uncertainties on her face and regretted his outburst. But he knew that to deny what he had uttered would be a lie, so he went on, this time more calmly, 'Akosua, I do not lie when I tell

38

you that in this world I bear nobody any grudge but one man. I am ready to forgive anybody who should harm me and apologise afterwards. Even if they do not apologise, I feel no hate. I do not hate the abrafo who beat me up in the temple, though I recognise some of them in the town, and I know myself to be in a position of influence to cause them severe harm. I do not hate those who enslaved me in Dagomba, nor those who dragged me through the jungle in a chaingang under such harsh conditions that many of us died on the way, to be buried in shallow graves. But this man Seku Wattara I have vowed to destroy, and this I shall do no matter the cost to me. I hate him only as a man can hate another he once loved with the deepest love.'

Akosua sealed her ears with her fingers, not wanting to hear any more. She walked slowly past him into the other room. As she reached out to open the door, he stopped her. On his face was the same hurt look as on hers; on his arm was her cloth. Her fingers were shaking so much that he had to help her wind the cloth round her body and fold it in place.

'Akosua,' he said, 'I know you think of your friend. Maybe you even admire her warrior-husband himself. I make a vow to destroy him, and I cannot step down. I am quite prepared to die afterwards. I know I shall not survive much longer because of his position in the society. I shall be killed as a criminal, but many years afterwards, perhaps my story will be remembered for what I intend to prove today – there is no escape from justice.'

Akosua had stood there meekly looking at the floor. When he was through with speaking she stepped quietly outside and left without a word. She disappeared through the door leading to the main entrance of the palace, and Jakpa stood staring at the spot for several moments. At last he closed the door, went and sat at his table and buried his head in his hands.

4

Seku was losing faith in fetish priests. For a whole week his house had been full of them and their attendants. They wore their usual straw skirts with talismans of leather, metal and shells around their necks, arms, wrists and legs, so that they clanged like bells as they danced, waving their 'bodua' of horse-tail, followed by attendants in white cloth who sprinkled white powder on their bodies. In the beginning all had been enthusiastic, but now they talked less of the power of their medicines, and concentrated on trying to find out the evil wizard or witch who had 'eaten' her soul. Unless this was done, they insisted, she couldn't be cured. They were referring to the Asante belief in 'abayie'. These 'abayie' were demons living in certain human bodies. At night they left the still-breathing body to go on their tours to devour the soul of some hapless victim for whom they bore a grudge. Unless the demon returned, the sleeping body never woke up. If on the other hand the body was moved away during the night, then the demon had no home unless it got it back. 'Abayie' were the cause of many mysterious deaths, and many of the fetish priests pressed Seku for information on any persons, particularly old women, who he felt had reason to bear him or his wife a grudge, but he couldn't help them.

One evening he unwittingly uttered his lack of confidence in their powers. It was a week after his hurried return from Sefwi, and most of the attending fetish priests were dancing in the open courtyard. Mbinge couldn't sleep through the din, of course, but she smiled bravely at him as he kept coming in and going out impatiently. He meant the words for himself, but his friend Ntiamoah's startled face made him realise that he had said them out aloud: 'Worthless deceivers of men, you dance and dance instead of curing the sick woman. I am not paying you to celebrate, but to work!' Two of the fetish priests were not dancing, and standing quite close, they had overheard him. The elderly one, with the hairs turning grey in his head, rebuked him gently, 'My son, this is no celebration we are conducting. Your woman's infection is the worst I have ever seen. I believe the Fulani used a poison that is unknown in this land. Before we can possibly cure her, we must speak to our fetishes and gods to beg them to invoke the help of the great Nyame, creator of all. We know of only one way to approach Him; it is an ancient ritual. If you should perhaps have more confidence in the methods of other men, by all means approach them. We can work together, or if you want, you can send us all away. The costs will certainly be heavy, but Otumfuor, himself a sick man, has assured you that he will settle half the fees.' He then walked off without giving Seku a chance to apologise, followed by the other, the only woman among the six fetish priests.

On the ninth day after his return Mbinge gave birth, several weeks earlier than was normal. Certainly, Seku was not expecting it. It was early in the morning, and he was sipping porridge in a calabash when a scream came from her room. He jumped and rushed there, pushing the attending women out of the way. The look on her face really terrified him. It was crossed with the deepest pain, and she was writhing from side to side. She had bitten her lips so hard that they were bleeding. There was an unpleasant smell in the little room, and he saw one old woman wiping his wife's bottom and legs. He felt anger and humiliation, but the fetish priestess took his hand, saying:

'You must leave, my lord. Her time has come.'

But he stubbornly refused to go, even though Mbinge's crying tore his heart. They took off all the clothes on her so that she lay stark naked on the mattress, then they ordered her to 'press'. At first only air came out from the other place, then Mbinge's cries took on a different note, and he saw a small black object forcing its way out between her legs and there was some blood because the woman's stretched vagina had got torn. He ran out and vomited his porridge in the courtyard.

Afterwards, they brought him the baby to see. It was a boy. The old woman said that it resembled Mbinge very much, but he could neither agree nor disagree. It looked like any other baby: fat, sleepy and so helpless. He gave the bundle of clothes and baby back to her and asked to see his wife. 'Later,' she replied. 'We must tidy up the place first.'

It was late afternoon before he knew. Ntiamoah had come to visit him. He had brought a special meal prepared by his Gonja wife, but Seku was too nervous to eat. The fetish priests had been called in by the priestess, who refused to admit Seku, even though he went on his knees before her and pressed his forehead on the ground at her feet. After a long time, it seemed to Seku, the priests came out one after the other, all

41

looking very gloomy. He ran up like an eager slave when the priestess gave a sign.

'It is very bad,' she said. 'There was a good chance that the herbs we had applied might cure her, but now the birth efforts have completely drained her strength.'

'Then it is finished?' he asked disbelievingly.

She looked at him, looked down, then looked him in the eyes. 'Our people have a saying: Nyame works in mysterious ways. What I know is, only He can save her now.'

She stepped aside and followed him in.

The room had been carefully tidied up, and there was nothing to suggest that a few hours before a birth had taken place there. Mbinge's bed-clothes had been changed. She was sleeping on her back, and on her face was such a childlike peace that he was very moved. She was wrapped up in white cloths. The old woman who had shown him the baby was sitting on the floor at her right side. The baby lay well-wrapped up on a mat at her left side.

He knelt down and took one of her hands in his. The baby suddenly cried, and a young woman whose presence Seku hadn't noticed picked it up and walked outside so that it would not disturb Mbinge's sleep. He covered up his wife's hand, and checked to see if the covering cloths were well wrapped round her. He sat there by her side for a long period in silence. Ntiamoah came when the fetish priestess allowed him to enter, and Seku nodded a silent greeting.

He approached the young woman with his son. She was sitting with another woman who was suckling his baby. 'Akosua,' he said to the first woman, 'I thank you for coming, and for bringing your maid as a wet-nurse for my wife's child. Your uncle, the respectable Nana Amoaten, has a fine niece.'

Akosua took the baby away from the wet-nurse and said, 'She has given you a fine son, Opanin Seku. He will grow to be as beautiful as his mother and as valiant as his father.'

Seku declined to take the child. 'It is hungry,' he said.

Ntiamoah had followed Seku, and he bent to tickle the child. 'A fine baby,' he said.

'What will you call him, Opanin Seku?' Akosua asked. 'It is customary that a child be named by the father within eight days of the birth, after consultations with his family and wife —'

She stopped, but the damage had been done. Akosua would have given all she had to have been able to take the words back. Seku's face

42

was without obvious emotion, indeed he even wore a smile.

'Call him Obonsam,*' he replied quietly. 'He has killed his mother.'

Mbinge died two nights later. It was approaching midnight, and the house was quiet and nearly empty. Four of the fetish priests had quietly left the home. They had lost hope that the woman could ever be saved. The birth efforts had rendered her weak, and the gangrenous wound had suddenly got worse, and it seemed no herbs or medicines could check the smell of rotting flesh. The Fulani's poison had strange powers indeed.

Most of the attending friends had stopped coming. They too could sense from the general atmosphere that the woman was doomed, and they couldn't bear to see her dying, so they had decided it would be better to prepare for the funeral afterwards. For such was the way of the Asante: they recognised the days of birth and of death as the most important in the life of a person, because they were the times when the person left the land of the dead for that of the living, and when the person left the living for the dead. A birth was often linked up with a long-ago death, for the Asante believed that dead ancestors rejoined the living in the form of a baby. But a death was regarded as the more important of the two prime occasions. It was all bound up in the religion. At the top the religion of the Asante (or Akan, for the Asante are only a small part of the Akan people) was Nyame, creator of all, so awesome and powerful that men couldn't directly deal with him. Under Nyame were the many idols and fetishes through whom one prayed to the great Nyame. These idols and fetishes could be approached directly only by fetish priests. Then there was the class of ancestors, or the dead, to whom one could directly appeal for help. Because the Asante believed that the dead never completely left the living, a dead body was treated with the utmost respect, and this was the reason why Mbinge's friends had gone home to make sure that their contributions to the funeral of the dying woman would not in any way fall short of what was normal.

Apart from the servants only Akosua, the wet nurse, and Fatima from Zongo were present on the evening of the death. Because she had lost her own child three weeks before, the wet-nurse felt strong bonds of affection for Mbinge's baby, and she was quite happy to be allowed to stay all day and night in the home. Fatima, Mbinge's closest friend in Kumasi, slept every evening in the home. Akosua alternated spending

* Satan.

43

the night in the sick woman's home with old Maame Ntosour. It was fate which chose that Mbinge's death should occur on the day she slept at the place.

Akosua had turned in rather early. It was horrible to sit near a friend who only two weeks before had been chattering and cheerful, and who now lay sleeping in a wakeless coma, dying slowly and peacefully. She shared the guest-room with Fatima, the wet nurse and the baby, a fortunate arrangement because she was afraid of the dark and of sleeping alone. She couldn't sleep. She lay there for several hours, listening to the gentle snoring of her companions, but a strange restlessness had seized her, and the sleep just wouldn't come.

Seku and his friend Ntiamoah were sitting round a fire in the middle of the courtyard. Ever since the birth, Seku had spent both nights sitting there waiting and waiting. His friend Ntiamoah, seeing his friend's suffering, had voluntarily joined him in his vigil: both men went to sleep for a few hours at dawn when the house woke up again.

Towards midnight, the fetish priestess stood in Mbinge's doorway. Both men immediately went up to her. She closed the door after them. Apart from Mbinge's sleeping mattress, there were two mats and blankets spread out on both sides of her: both the priestess and remaining priest spent the night with their patient. The disorder of the sleeping places betrayed the haste with which they had been left. The priest was on his knees by Mbinge's side, his hands on the mattress but not touching her. Mbinge, was, as usual, covered with white cotton cloths, but she was not lying as peaceful as always. She seemed to be choking for air, her whole body quivered, but she didn't kick out, nor did she utter a sound. Seku knelt down beside her and put a hand lightly on her cheek. The gesture seemed to calm the woman for a few moments, then she suddenly jerked, Seku's hand slipped into her mouth and the teeth snapped, giving him a nasty gash. Instinctively he took his hand away, before he allowed it to settle on her cheek again. She lay breathing deeply, and he ran his fingers gently over her face. She took a deep breath, and her whole body shuddered, then she lay still. The tears rolled silently down Seku's cheeks.

The priestess touched Seku's shoulder gently. 'It is over, my lord. It would be best if you left us alone to see to the rest.'

The two men went and sat down by the fire outside. Ntiamoah said viciously, 'Sepo! Sepo! I shall use all my influence to have that Fulani tortured brutally to death, else do not call me again Ntiamoah of Pataase!'

44

Seku's face was like that of a man in deep sorrow. He did not answer.

Ntiamoah went on, 'His feet and arms will be bound to a chair, a dagger shall be run through his cheeks and tongue, the skin on his back will be cut off and shown to him. He shall eat his own eye, the left one, yes! and his balls too, yes, they shall be shoved down his throat, else I am not Ntiamoah of Pataase! Cowards die the way they deserve. What valour is there in ambushing a pregnant woman?'

'Let us not talk of it, Yaw,' Seku replied at last. 'It is over.'

'No, Seku, it is only beginning. For him it is only about to begin, I assure you. Why, I'll even ask that his whole family be damned, too!'

'What is the use, my brother? It won't bring her back.'

'True, but he must suffer the hurt he has caused.'

'I killed his brother. Have you forgotten?'

'It was an accident. I was an eyewitness. But, by the gods above, Seku, don't you want revenge?'

'Yes, Yaw, I do. But leave his family out of it, else it will never stop.'

Ntiamoah shook his head. 'You are a strange one, Seku. When you returned from Sefwi, you were a wild man. You nearly killed that Fulani with your hands, and I was certain you would have killed those guards if they had tried to stop you. Yet now that you certainly have a definite reason to have the man and his family tortured to painful death, you speak like a woman.'

Seku looked at him again, searchingly. 'Yaw, in the past few days I've done a lot of thinking. My mind has gone over many things in my life, and I find it hard to involve the innocent family of the Fulani in this affair. Besides, you know it is a law that only a man, and none of his relatives or friends, can be held responsible for his actions.'

'It is a law of Asante for Asante, my brother. The Fulani are not among our number.'

'But they are guests in Asante. Their representatives will approach the king for mercy on his family, and he could hardly refuse unless he wants to cut off trade with the Hausa and Fulani.'

'You are a pessimist, my brother. Asante laws against law-breakers are harsh. The Fulani leaders themselves will seek to avoid entering this highly emotional crime and trial.'

'Once, my brother Yaw, you asked me to tell you a story. It was a story about my relationship with Mbinge, and the place was at your house, during your celebrations after our safe return from the Gyaaman campaign. Do you remember?'

'I do. I also remember you refused to disclose the secret.'

45

'The time was not right. At another moment, I would have told you, but not during a drunken feast.'

'Is this moment the right one?'

'I want you to know this, Yaw. I love Mbinge more than anything else. For many years she has been the centre of my life. Everything I did, I did for her. When I hunted, I thought of the money the meat would bring for us to live together. When I fought for Asante, I dreamt of her living in a decent home with servants to serve her. When I refused the approaches of other women, I thought of a vow I had made before her. Now she is no longer there, and I do not see clearly. I do not feel a reason to continue. It seems the world is stopping for me, my brother.'

'Do not talk of death, Seku —'

'I do not talk of suicide, my brother. I just want to explain my story to you. You have often expressed your admiration for Mbinge's beauty. Do you know where she comes from? Do you know what she was before she decided to leave her home to accompany me?'

'I do not know, Seku.'

'Then listen, Yaw. In the land of the Mossi there is a little village called Kumbili, renowned for its sewing of smocks. Her father was chief there. He had many wives and many beautiful daughters, but Mbinge was the pick of the lot. Her mother was a Frafra slave who gave her the name Mbinge, but the chief loved this wife above all others, and he had big plans for his most beautiful daughter. You know of Wagadugu, capital of the Mossi? It lies far to the north of Kumbili, and its beauty and size equals that of Kumasi. The King of Mossi had many sons, and one of them once visited the village to check up on taxes according to the will of his father. That was many years ago, and Mbinge was only a child, yet the man made his approaches to the father, who was only too happy to betrothe her to the rich prince on the black horse. Yet as you now see, she left him for me.'

Ntiamoah nodded silently. He now began to understand his friend's passionate love for his wife. He knew that the Mossi followed a patrilineal system, so that a woman was much less emancipated than her Asante counterpart. For the woman to have gone against her parent's wishes must have demanded a great determination and love from her part.

'Yaw, my brother,' Seku went on, 'I had a brother younger than I, but with more sense in his head. I taught him how to ride a horse, but after I had taught him all I knew, he was better. I taught him to shoot the bow, and he did it better than I. I taught him wrestling and sword fighting, till he was among the best in the whole village, though he was much thinner and lighter than most men. I loved my brother, Yaw.'

'He is the brother you told me about at the feast?'

'He is the same. Yaw. A man far better than I. He should have lived instead of I, but great Nyame is not always just. Once I should have died, but Nyame let my brother save my life. The lion is the king of the plains; the only being it considers its equal is man, and it prefers to leave him in peace. But every once in a while the king of beasts forgets its limits, then it will steal the livestock of its only rival, man. Once such an event occurred soon after I had reached my full manhood, and I was among the seven youths chosen to track down the cattle-killer and to destroy it. The lion is a shrewd animal. It knows that men will hunt it if it steals their cattle, so it tries to cross its spoor with those of similarly sized lions. For a long distance we followed the killer, then there arose an argument when it carefully followed the spoor of another lion. Where the two tracks parted, we stood arguing about which track was the right one. Instead of going together to inspect just one spoor then the next, we foolishly agreed to part in two groups, and my group had three members only whilst the other group had four. We came to some thickets, and our leader warned us to be careful. Even then, the lion was quicker. There was suddenly a short deep roar, and a black-maned flash from the tall grass was the first thing I saw, then there was a short cry and the crunching of bones, and our leader was dead. Being the youngest in the line, I was last, and this saved my life. As it sprang and brought down my remaining companion, I threw my spear, aiming at the chest, but the metal embedded itself in the lion's soft stomach. It crashed the man's head with a bite and made for me. I drew my sword and held my shield, but against a mad wounded lion these tools are nearly useless. True I have killed a leopard armed with only a sword, but the weapon for the lion is the spear. It is held propped up on the ground at an angle so that the wildly attacking beast impales itself, and can then be finished off with a sword, this method being possible only for lions which tend to act blindly when angry, trusting in their strength as they do. With my sword I had no chance and I knew it. Great was thus my surprise when it suddenly checked itself and sank onto the ground, dead. I knew it wasn't my spear which had done it, and I turned and saw my brother adjusting his bow. He had secretly followed us, against custom, for he was under age, yet he had saved my life. Yes, Yaw, I loved my brother dearly.'

He suddenly got up and went to fetch wood from the kitchen and supplied the dying fire with more fuel.

'It is getting cool, Yaw. A fire like this must never be allowed to die. Fire is a strange thing, but it is not only wood that burns. Sometimes a man too burns with pain and confusion in his heart. I should hate you, Yaw. You and I should be enemies, yet we fought hand in hand, back to back in Gyaaman.'

Ntiamoah looked deeply shocked. 'I do not understand, Seku,' he stammered.

'I am Gonja, Yaw. I never told you this before, but my father was a young man when Asante sacked Gonja. He was a bitter man, because his father had been court record-keeper before him, and had told him much of the old glories of Gonja which had been destroyed by all-powerful Asante. He brought us up, my brother and I, to hate Asante and to remember the evil done to our people with slavery. He taught us the rudiments of Arabic, but I never had a head for learning, so that my father and I never fully saw eye to eye. Finally I gave up learning, for which he never quite forgave me, the poor man. But I shall be fair and say that before he died he gave me his blessing, even if I did not show Allah the respect He deserved by reading about Him. My brother, on the other hand, was the pride of my father. He was a natural genius, and while still young he greatly surprised an Alhaji from Zaria in Hausaland. An Alhaji is no small man, Yaw. He is a dedicated Moslem who has visited Mecca to pray. This man was so delighted that he made my brother a present of a horse, young as he was. Asante prides herself on the learned secretaries in the king's court at Kumasi. Yet were my brother alive today, they would appear as children before his great knowledge of the Koran.'

Ntiamoah asked, 'Did your father take you to Mossi?'

Seku shook his head. 'We were born there. His father and his two wives were killed in the final storming of the town by Asante troops, and he fled to Mossi, which he felt, correctly as it turned out, would be safe from further Asante attack. Several years later he sent back two loyal servants to arrange a marriage for him to a young girl whose family he had known, and he treasured us, the two children she gave him, above all others because we were full-blooded Gonja.'

'I am sorry, Seku,' Ntiamoah said. 'I know Asante has done a great wrong to many peoples, but I cannot stop it, however much I would like to. I am deeply moved to find that you, my best friend, whom I love more than my own brothers, should have been so affected by the

48

warriors of my people. I hope you will find it in your heart to forgive me this wrong done to your people by mine, and that you will help me find a solution to the problem.'

'Don't take it so hard,' was Seku's reply. 'I have often told you that we are brothers, and the words were from my heart. I love you as a brother. Nor do I blame Asante; those days are past. Since my arrival in Asante I see more clearly that there are hands stronger than those of Asante behind this evil. I agree with my father that slavery is evil, but I disagree with him when he puts Asante directly responsible. Asante does what she does only because of fear.'

'I am glad you do not hate me, my brother Seku.'

'We are brothers, Yaw. You now play the role of my brother who is dead. When you asked me to come with you as best man to ask for the hand of your Gonja wife, I was deeply touched. It went far beyond the bonds of ordinary friendship. Yaw, once my brother did the same thing for me, so I was glad to repay this action, even if in an indirect fashion. I remember the day as if it were yesterday. The chief was sitting on a lion skin in his room smoking a pipe. On either side of him sat two of his favourite wives on goat-skins. The man was wearing a striped black and white smock with white trousers and a flattish hat, whilst his women had yellow cloths on. He bade us welcome and servants brought us skins to sit on. After a suitable time had passed he asked what had brought us to him, and my brother spoke for me.

' "Great one," he said, "we know you to be a busy man, so we shall not waste your time and we shall come to the point. My brother Seku and I have come to let you know that your daughter's manners and looks have caused us to approach you to let you know that we should like to consider marriage, with your approval."

'The chief knew which of us wanted his daughter, since I did not speak a word. But he said, "Which daughter, young men? I have fourteen wives and countless children, some old enough to be your parents, some young enough to be your children. I liked and respected your father very much. His passing away six months ago leaves our village sadder than it used to be, because he was a learned Moslem, and though we Mossi are not Moslem, yet we respect these men of iron discipline. Speak my young friends."

'But when my brother mentioned Mbinge's name, the man turned quickly away. "No, my children," he said, "not that one. Chose any other but her." He then told us the story of Mbinge's betrothal to the prince from Wagadugu, and invited us again to consider any other of his

49

daughters. The chief was a kind man, Yaw, my brother. He respected my father, and he admired us his sons for our courage and boldness, but he had his plans and ambitions, which did not directly include me. He tactfully gave us many presents and even insisted that we eat with him so that there would be no disgrace in his having turned down our proposal. But my heart was torn, for I hadn't known of Mbinge's engagement, and I had hoped to win her.'

'Then you had known her for long?'

'We grew up in the same village, Yaw. You can say I loved her from childhood. When I went to call her to play, her mother playfully called us husband and wife. Later on, as our ways became more separated because we were approaching maturity, I still lingered round the stream at the times when the girls went to fetch water. But I didn't know how much she loved me till two incidents occurred. First, after the incident with the lion. She showed more concern over me than over any of the others, and inspected me carefully to make sure I hadn't even been scratched. Finally when my father died, she confessed her love for me. It is difficult to be alone in the world, Yaw, especially when one depends so much on another as we did on our iron-willed old man. It was easy to quarrel with him, yet once he was gone, a big gap came to our lives. In any patrilineal system, a father's death is heavy and unbearable, and ours was made worse by the fact that he had made us aware of our isolation by repeatedly reminding us that we were Gonja and not Mossi. My brother seemed even more hurt than I, so that I was afraid to discuss my sorrow with him. Finally I decided to waylay Mbinge by the stream and tell her of my unhappiness. Surely she would understand, for I had played with her as a child. The first time I approached her at dawn, she was afraid, but she soon saw I was only unhappy and tried her best to comfort me. It was then I realised that she also loved me, and when I asked, she confirmed it.'

'Seku my brother, forgive this question, for it is foolish: why did she not tell you of her betrothal, or did she not know?'

Seku nodded and smiled gently, 'Yes she knew, Yaw. She told me afterwards why she didn't tell me. It was because it was many years since the prince had called, and she believed and hoped that he had lost interest, since he didn't even send servants regularly to check up on her health and to make presents. Besides, she loved me, and wanted me.'

'So what happened, my brother Seku?'

'I got ill, Yaw, so ill that everybody thought I would die. They fetched many herbalists, but none could cure me, since it was love which was breaking me. The face I yearned to see most of all never came, for Mbinge's father, still hopeful of marrying his daughter to power, had banned her from seeing me. My brother was afraid I would die. He got thin and sat by my side thinking and thinking. Finally one day he said, "Brother Seku, I see only one solution – elopement. Get well, and we shall leave this village."

' "Where do we go, brother?" I asked. "This is our only home." "No," he replied. "This is only our temporary home. Remember what father always told us? Let us go to Gonja and rebuild our nation."

' "Asante is too strong," I said with resignment in my voice but hope in my heart.

' "Then we shall not work in the Gonja palace. We have hands and can farm. Come, brother Seku, get well. Gonja waits for us."

'That day I ate my biggest meal for many weeks. My brother got into contact with the girl, and when I learned that she was also prepared to elope, I was out of bed within three days, and had almost fully recovered within a week. My brother's plan was simple. We would sneak out at night and ride to the Sisili river, a full two days' journey. From there we would continue by boat in the broad swift river, which the Mossi couldn't cross with horses because of crocodiles. Not very far down the river were the first settlements of Dagomba, a subject state of Asante where the Mossi wouldn't dare follow. My brother left a week before the great day to prepare the boat in the right place, and when he returned after four days a sudden thought occurred to me and I asked, "My brother, in Gonja we cannot carry out our father's ideals. It will be a big disappointment for father if we should end up not organising war to liberate our people as he had always wished."

'My brother was silent for several moments. I knew the bonds he had felt to father, the great desire of his to follow the dead man's ideals. He replied simply, "We shall watch and see." But I knew the sacrifice he was making because of me, a sacrifice which would never have given him peace of mind again if he were still alive today. I loved my brother, Yaw, and he loved me very much.'

He bent and arranged the wood, so that the fire spurted again, with crackling sounds. An owl hooted far away, but otherwise Aboaba at night was as silent as always. There was a half-moon, but the clouds were dark and thick, so that the moon was much less bright than it should have been. Ntiamoah glanced around the courtyard. Only Mbinge's room had a light; he could faintly discern the figures of the fetish priests quietly attending the dead woman, whose form he was relieved not to see through the curtains of the opened doorway. One of the other doors was open slightly. He couldn't see clearly who it was leaning against the doorway, but he guessed that one of the women had overheard the news of death and was both too shy or saddened to approach Seku and much too afraid to go back to bed. He turned his attention back to Seku, and waited for him to continue.

'Yaw, my brother,' Seku said in his deep voice. 'My brother's plan worked wonderfully. Mbinge met us at the appointed spot, and we had two horses at our disposal, Mbinge and I rode the leading horse with my brother bringing up the rear on his. We were happy, Mbinge and I, and though afraid of being followed, the next morning we were sure we were far enough away, and began to cheer up. Mbinge wept as she thought of her mother and brothers and sisters, but I was happy to get her away from her unknown prince. We slackened our pace. This was a foolish mistake. Unknown to us the chief's daughters had told their mother of Mbinge's absence, and soon after we had started, there was a big alarm in the whole village. All our best friends were questioned, and one of them was forced to confess that in a long-ago conversation with my brother, my brother had mentioned the stream Sisili as the surest way for a man escaping from Dagomba to Mossi, or from Mossi to Dagomba. So the next morning a large expedition of horsemen was sent off after us. We were aware of being chased on the second afternoon. We had camped on a little hill for lunch when my brother pointed at a faint cloud of dust far away. At first I thought it was the wind, or maybe a pack of wild dogs, but after listening with our ears close to the ground, we became certain they were horses. We rode away as fast as we could, but our horses were tired, and more there were two of us, Mbinge and I, on one of them. My brother could have ridden away to safety, leaving us to our fate, but this he did not do. Once our horse slipped and nearly fell, and he made us change mounts. All the time the horsemen came closer. At last we saw the river ahead, broad and brown. We went to look for the canoe hidden in the reeds, and by this time the Mossi were nearly upon us. I covered Mbinge with my shield and pressed her to the bottom of the canoe. My brother protected me with his shield as I pushed the canoe into deeper waters, then, god of gods, he gave a cry and staggered three steps away from me, from the river. He had been hit! I hesitated a split second: the men were now two hundred steps away, and storming like the wind. My mind was torn between two choices – who should I save, my brother or my woman? Yaw, I loved my brother, but I also loved Mbinge! A second arrow hit my brother, he fell, and I pushed the boat further into the river, running away. My brother lifted his head in disbelief – Yaw, I see his face, I see the shock, the pain, the disappointment! He was my younger brother, yet he had done so much for me. He had saved me from a lion, he had got me the woman of my heart, and I could only repay him with treachery. He called out once, "My brother Seku!" then another arrow hit his leg and he lay there. I paddled away, my eyes fixed on the scene. Only the gods saved my life, for though many arrows were shot, the nearest one got stuck in the canoe near my leg, and one pierced one of the paddles I was using to steer the boat. I think of this event, Yaw, and my heart bleeds. I have never forgotten that day, and I never shall. It is the day of my greatest shame, and often have I wished that I had died there.'

Ntiamoah was silent. He put more wood on the fire, and still felt uncertain how to phrase any question he had in mind. He was very moved by Seku's sorrow. A man can take only so much before he breaks, and it seemed Seku had had much more unpleasant experiences than most men he knew of.

'You know the rest of my story, Yaw,' Seku went on. 'Mbinge and I escaped to Dagomba, where we managed to bribe our way to free access to Salaga, where we stayed for several months. In Salaga, Mbinge had a miscarriage. It was also in Salaga that I swore my oath never to touch any woman other than her. It seemed only fair – I had sacrificed my brother for her, Yaw, and I loved my brother dearly.'

'But Seku – your brother, did he die from the wounds at the river?' Ntiamoah asked.

'No, Yaw,' replied Seku. 'I knew my brother was alive as I paddled away. I saw him being lifted up and his hands tied. I saw the men hit him till he collapsed, and I wanted to jump into the water to die with him. The tears rolled down my cheeks. But I heard Mbinge's sobbing, and I thought it would be better if I stayed. I got to know how my brother died only during the Gyaaman war. You remember the Gonja man I killed? He is the very one who betrayed my brother. He belonged to the only other Gonja family in Kumbili, and he had rivalled my brother's learning in Arabic. He was also interested in fighting against Asante, but I do not know how he joined the Gyaaman army. He told me my brother was kept alive for three months, then after there was no hope of my ever coming back, he was stoned to death. I loved my brother, Yaw, yet I caused him this shameful and painful death.'

He was silent for several moments then he went on, his voice heavy with hopelessness, 'Now I am alone in the world. The only woman I have ever loved too has left me. Now I think back to the time my brother was captured. I wish great Nyame would only give me back these few moments in time. I have had many years to think it over, and I know that I should have died with my brother. It is only just for one who had loved me so much. As for Mbinge, by now she might have forgotten all about me and would be quite happy in her prince's home in Wagadugu. I have brought them both violent death, the two persons I loved most of all.'

'She left you a son, Seku. Love him as they loved you.'

'I shall do my best, Yaw, my brother, but I wish it had not been there. Much as I love its mother, I know it will serve to remind me daily of the pain in my heart. I wish I could die, Yaw, and end my troubles. The baby will serve to anchor me firmly to a life I would rather leave. I truly wish it had not been born. I know I speak like a coward, but I wish I could die and leave all my troubles behind.'

The two men sat there in silence. The fire crackled and sputtered and died slowly, but neither seemed to notice or to care. Seku sat with his arms on his knees, his eyes with a faraway look. Ntiamoah had his head resting in the palm of a hand whose elbow was propped up on his knees. He was suddenly afraid that his friend might choose to commit suicide, and he felt saddened because he might not be able to console him.

Akosua stood there in the doorway, and her eyes were wet. She had overheard the story of her friend's death and overheard also the story of Seku. She felt very sorry for him. Her mind went back to Jakpa. She still didn't appreciate who he was – perhaps a friend of Seku's brother who had sworn to avenge his death. She felt afraid and sad. Though she had left Jakpa in anger the day he had told her he wanted to kill Seku, nevertheless she had gone to nurse Mbinge as he had suggested. She tried to give herself excuses for her decision – after all Mbinge was a good friend of hers – and she tried to convince herself that she had done it from her own conscience and would have done it anyway without his suggesting it. She didn't know whether to hate him or not. He seemed to have a strange power over her that she did not understand.

A cock crowed, to be followed by other cocks from far and near. It was approaching dawn. One of the two other women in the room asked Akosua sleepily if anything was wrong. It was the wet nurse. When Akosua told her it was over, she sat upright in the dark room, as if petrified with shock. Then she clutched the baby to her breast and began to weep loudly. Fatima woke up, and soon all three women were wailing. The servants also woke up, and the house was loud with lamentations. Only the fetish priests and Seku and Ntiamoah looked on with dry eyes. At sunrise Maame Ntosuor arrived, and when they told her, she led the wailing people to inspect the body. The fetish priests approached Seku and Ntiamoah, and servants were sent out to far and near to inform friends of the incident. Of the women only Maame Ntosuor and the fetish priestess seemed to have their wits around them. They ordered the others to warm up water to bathe the body, and they tidied up the room and changed the bedding for the very best Seku had.

Soon after dawn the body of the dead woman was laid in state. She was dressed up in her finest white cloths, and the body was well powdered and perfumed. They put the best gold decorations on the walls of the room, and they laid by the side of the body a parcel containing sandals, bathing and cooking utensils, gold, spoons and all other necessities she might need in the land of the dead. The woman wore all her best golden earrings, necklaces and arm bands, and her eyes were closed as if she were only sleeping peacefully. Fatima went home to put on her mourning cloths. The people prepared seats for the chief-mourners in the room with the body: for Fatima her best friend and for Seku her husband near the doorway. Seku went to bath, put on his black mourning cloth and took his seat.

The first guests began arriving soon after. They all came barefoot to give respect to the deceased one, and they wore black Kuntunkuni or the red Kobin funeral cloths. The men came to wish Seku courage and to offer condolence. The women burst into wild songs of sorrow and wept loudly. All the guests were meant to take a look at the body. They shook hands with Fatima at the doorway before they passed her to look at the body. On their way back they greeted Seku and offered condolence. The wailing songs of the women gave the place a sad atmosphere. Those who had known her best sang songs as they beheld the body. Ntiamoah was most moved by Fatima's first wail:

'My beautiful sister, feeder of my children, can it be that you should go before me? What will happen to my children who call you their second mother? Will there be another lady ever to pass by and offer them beancakes? Will another woman give them cloth to cover their bodies at night? How can you leave us now, sister? Did we wrong you? I love you, my sister, and my heart is empty and sad. I remember your days at Zongo in the same house as I. I remember how noble you were, how you looked after my children when I was away, how you helped me with my washing and housework, though I am hardly fit to wipe your feet, oh beautiful one! What of Seku your husband? Must he be left to face the world alone now, he who has loved you so faithfully and truly? He who spurns all other women because of you, refusing even a second wife? What of your son, so young and so helpless and innocent? Must he grow up on the milk of strangers? Must he never know how sweet and good his mother was? Must he endure the teasing children when they call him motherless? Must he be fed by strangers all his life? Oh, my beautiful sister, the Great One has called you at a very unfortunate time. Oh my sister, we are sad and broken in spirit!'

So she wept, and Maame Ntosuor led her away to recover. She had got up from her seat to address the body, and in her absence it was occupied by Akosua, who shook hands with the guests coming in to look at the body. Many seats had been hurriedly arranged in the compound yard and the place was crowded with people. Servants had been sent for alcohol, and most of the men were getting drunk. The wiser ones, though, drank only little. According to tradition, those partaking in a funeral ate only before dawn and again after sunset. Those who had not eaten when they heard the news had to fast till evening, and the foolish ones drank heavily to hide their hunger, with the result that many often went to the bathroom to vomit. There was a band playing drums and blowing horns, but this first celebration of the funeral was only to give the dead body respect and a decent burial. The proper funeral followed after forty days of the death, and this was the more important occasion. At this time the mourners finally reconciled themselves to their loss. The alcohol flowed like water, and many mourning dances were performed.

The body was never left alone during the whole two days it lay in state. There were always at least two people to keep it 'company', and even at night Maame Ntosuor and Fatima stayed awake when Seku could keep his eyes no longer open. Ntiamoah had been watching over his friend carefully and he was relieved to see him comporting himself so well. Seku greeted the guests very friendly, and he showed no exaggerated emotion. His eyes seemed far away, and sometimes he smiled to himself, as if remembering some happy times with the woman. He even played once with his new-born son, tickling him till he smiled. But his eating habits worried Ntiamoah a little. Seku ate only once a day, and even then only a few bites. Ntiamoah was hopeful it would improve after some time – after all, the man and his wife had dearly loved each other, and it was normal that he should starve himself when she died.

In the evening of the first day they got word from the king. He sent two senior linguists to offer condolence, and they said the royal weavers would provide a kyenkyen cloth the next day for the burial. They didn't stay as long as the other mourners did, and excused themselves and left. Seku and Ntiamoah had already ordered a good burial cloth, but they sent to stop work on it, sure that the king's weavers would provide a matchless specimen.

Ntiamoah had thought of a place for the body to be buried. He had first considered his family's own personal burial place, but had decided against asking his uncle's permission. For the people of Asante, dead ancestors were very special. The senior families had their own graveyards where their dead were buried, and each year offerings of food were made to the ancestors. His uncle would most certainly have refused to allow the dead woman to be buried in his family graveyard: the ancestors would have objected to a stranger amongst their midst, and would perhaps send disease or misfortune to punish the living. So he had suggested to Seku that the body be buried near Aboabo. The cemetery there was not as ancient as many of the others in Kumasi, and it was there that strangers were normally buried. Ntiamoah arranged for an area away from the poorer corners where commoners were buried, choosing a spot near the burial place of nobles and high officials from other lands who had died while on an errand to Kumasi.

One of the most senior men to attend the funeral was Nana Abinowa, Ntiamoah's uncle. He approached Seku and tried to console him, saying, 'Courage, my son. We of Asante believe that great Nyame gives each person two souls. When we die, one soul dies for all time, but the other returns to Nyame, who may decide with time to send it back to the land of the living again. Do not grieve too much. Even if our beloved sister does not return soon to rejoin us in life, we must remember that she is with Nyame, and it is rather she who weeps for us, and will help us if we pray to her.

'Let me tell you a story. Once Nyame lived very close to men, but pestles used to pound fufu annoyed Him, so He decided to move far into the heavens. The people got desperate upon seeing His departure. One old woman hit upon a solution; she collected all the mortars the people had, and they arranged them one on top of the other. You know what a mortar is: it is carved from a thick, short tree trunk, and fufu is pounded in it, but this old woman tried to use it as a bridge from earth to heaven, from man to Nyame. And she nearly succeeded: only one more mortar was needed, but they had no more. Somebody suggested removing one of the lowest mortars to add to the top, but of course the whole set came tumbling down, killing many people. I tell this story to illustrate that Nyame is withdrawn and is much too great to mix with ordinary living men. We of Asante worship many idols and fetishes, but they all draw their powers from Nyame, who prefers to watch and to wait. The dead lead a much more exalted life than we still on earth: they are close to the greatest Being of all time, and it is not we who should weep for them, but they for us, seeing our sins and greed. Courage, my son. She is better off than we are.'

That evening was the last before the burial. There was a wake-keeping from night to dawn, and many guests joined Seku in the courtyard before the room where the body lay. The women included Fatima, Akosua, Maame Ntosuor, Ntiamoah's wives and several others and they hummed songs all night long. Sometimes some of the men joined in the music, but most of the time they sat there silently, drinking hot gulps of akpeteshie gin and getting themselves drunk. They all felt hungry, but none complained, or stole away to fill his stomach. The wake-keeping was a solemn occasion to keep the body company for the last time. After this, no one would see the face and flesh of the woman any more. After this day Mbinge would be only a memory.

5

Jakpa was sitting outside the eastern side of the palace where the numerous chickens of the king and of some of his attendants were pecking grass and seeds. He was aware of the door being closed, and he turned curiously, expecting to see one of the palace eunuchs with left-overs from lunch for the birds. It was late afternoon, but the sun was still hot and bright, and he was happy that there were leafy trees under which one could shelter outside the palace.

It was Akosua. She wore black mourning cloths, her feet were bare on the ground, and her eyes looked red and swollen with crying, though they were dry now. He got up to demonstrate his welcome, but waited for her to speak first.

'They told me you were here,' she said simply, without first giving the customary greeting.

'I was watching the chickens. You remember the two hens your uncle's wives gave me? Well they've hatched eggs several times now, and I have many chickens. Look at that one – it is one of the first two, yes – the one with chicks. I can't see the other one...'

He put a hand above his eyes to shade them from the sun and looked through the many groups of chickens, trying to find where the hen was, but without luck. Akosua seemed uninterested, so he said, 'I can't find it, but it doesn't matter. Come, my sister. Let me offer you kola in my humble room.'

They went indoors to his room. When he shut the door she said: 'We had the burial today.'

He nodded. 'Yes, I'd heard of it.'

He dusted his best stool and set it behind her, but she didn't sit. He offered kola but she refused, and he remembered the fasting laws of funerals and cursed himself.

'I am glad you have come, my sister.'

'We had the burial today,' she repeated.

'Tell me of it, Akosua,' he suggested. 'Were there many people?'

She nodded, but didn't speak. It seemed to her that the whole of

59

Aboabo had attended the burial. The house had been crowded so densely that going across the courtyard was a real problem, and there were numerous other mourners outside as well. There had been a last great wailing as the body was lifted from the mattress, and they had followed the procession to the burial place. Many important people had come: there were linguists from the palace, and some of the lesser chiefs who had known Seku personally had attended.

One particular man of rank who had taken part in the Gyaaman campaign and had recommended Seku to the Asantehene had done something that had turned Seku's face hard and somewhat disrespect-ful, and though Seku had smiled politely before excusing himself, Akosua had sensed his anger. The old warrior had said, 'Young man, I offer my consolations. Your wife was a beautiful and respectable woman and all those who knew her loved her. I know the sorrow in your heart to be heavy, but there are many other women still living, and you will surely find one soon to care for your son.'

'I hear she was buried at the cemetery behind Aboabo.' Jakpa went on.

She began to cry. She had wept so often that now no tears came, just the sounds and the creasing of the face. He gently forced her to sit, but she continued crying. She continually dabbed at her face with the ends of her funeral cloth. The scenes came before her, the long procession to the cemetery, the drums and flutes and the wailing women. None of the men had cried, but they had been silent and their eyes had been red. She had watched Seku through her tears and wails. He had been very drunk, and he had been belching continuously. Most of the men wore hard faces full of hate for the evil murderer, but not Seku. It seemed that at last the full impact of the death had hit him. Alcohol made a man more light-headed, but Seku's face had been like that of a lost child. He had walked very closely by the men bearing the bundle of kyenkyen cloth, covering the entire body of the dead woman, and his eyes were fixed all the time on the ground just before him. He had given only one cry, 'Mbinge,' and uttered some Mossi words nobody had understood as the body was lowered into the grave. The fetish priestess had then stepped forward and addressed the spirit of the dead woman thus: 'Our sister Mbinge the beautiful, you are leaving us today: we have given you a sheep offering: we have performed your funeral. You go to take your place by the Supreme Being: do not let any of us get ill. Protect the health of your husband and son, remember your friends. Grant us all good health and long life, make sure we prosper.' Actually a blood relation should have spoken these words, according to tradition, but Mbinge was a stranger in Kumasi, and her husband had seemed too stunned to speak sensibly. As they covered up the body, Seku had turned suddenly and wept like a boy on his friend Ntiamoah's chest. Ntiamoah's voice had been thick and unclear as he tried to utter words of comfort, and Akosua had seen that he too was weeping like a child.

'Do not cry, Akosua. We must consider that she didn't suffer much.'

She sniffed and blew her nose, then she said, 'I feel sorry for the child.'

'It will not remember, Akosua. It will grow up and become a healthy boy.'

'I remember the wail of Fatima, her Hausa friend. She said, "Must you always be fed by strangers? Must you never see your mother's face?"'

He was silent.

'I fear for the baby, Jakpa. Serwaa, one of the maids at my home, is wet nurse for the baby. I was with her the day he was born, and when we tried to give the father his baby, he cursed him and said he had killed his mother. Do you think he will soften?'

'Yes, Akosua, I am sure. He loved her very much, and he won't harm him because of her.'

'I feel sorry for Nana Seku, too.'

He had no answer for that.

'He seems so lost, almost like a child. He seldom drank before, but now he practically lives on alcohol.'

'It will pass,' he interrupted. 'I think it is natural for a man to feel his wife's passing away.'

'I didn't know they had so few friends – I mean close friends. I was surprised to see them come to depend so much on Maame Ntosuor and me.'

'I don't understand. I heard that many people came.'

'Yes, but they only came because of his rank. I was even among those who welcomed the guests to the room.'

'I see.'

'Jakpa.'

'Yes.'

'Nana Seku – I overheard him tell Ntiamoah his story.'

He looked hard at her, then pulled a seat for himself facing her.

'Who are you, Jakpa?' she asked. 'Where did you meet them?'

'Did he not say?'

'He never mentioned you.'

'Seku had a brother.'

'He is dead,' she replied.

'Did he tell you how?'

'He wasn't speaking to me. It was his friend he spoke to, and I overheard their conversation.'

'Did he tell you how he left his brother to his fate?'

She nodded. 'He seems to have regretted it, Jakpa. He kept saying, "I wish I could get those few moments in time again. I have had many years to think it over, and I know I should have died with him at the Sisili river."'

'It is easy to weep over a decision in the past. It is easy to tell others you would do something when the opportunity will never arise again.'

'I believed him.'

He was suddenly furious. 'Because you are a woman,' he said coldly, 'and women have empty heads.'

'No, Jakpa. We are no more stupid than men. We are only different, that is all. A woman is a mother, and she has love and understanding. A man is foolish – he thinks of what other man think of him. Even if he can't afford it, he will wear the best cloths and throw big feasts to hide his poverty. A woman often sees more correctly than a man does.'

'It is not only women who love and try to understand men, Akosua. Sometimes a man also loves another man more than he loves a woman, and I am not talking of sick men who love boys as women.'

'You knew Nana Seku very well?'

'Don't call him, Nana, Akosua. It annoys me.'

'How should I call him, then, Kramo?'

'Don't call me Kramo either. He doesn't deserve the honorary title of Nana, that is all.'

'It is your opinion, Jakpa. I have my own mind.'

He got up and went to his sleeping room, taking some sheets of paper with him. Akosua waited a few moments for his return, but he didn't come back. She got up from her stool and pushed the make-shift raffia curtains to one side. He was lying in bed, pretending to read, but the frown on his face betrayed that he couldn't concentrate.

'Did you know him well, Jakpa?'

He rolled off the bed and deposited the papers on the neck of a clay water bottle. He pushed past her in the little doorway, and she thought he was going outside. But at the outer door he turned and replied, 'I thought I knew him, Akosua, but I was wrong. I thought I understood him thoroughly, but I was wrong.'

'Were you a friend of his brother's?'

'Did he say his brother had friends? Did he mention names?'

She nearly said no, then remembered the incident Seku had told of in Gyaaman. 'He only mentioned that a friend of his brother had betrayed them.'

'The friend was first brutally tortured. But how did he know? The friend lives in Mossi.'

'They met in Gyaaman, and —'

'Gyaaman!' He stepped forward, his eyes wide open with surprise. 'Akosua, are you sure?'

'That is what he said. You knew this friend well?'

'Yes, Akosua. He was a brave man. He did what he had always said he would, and deserves respect.'

'Nana Seku killed him because the man told him his brother was dead.'

Jakpa looked at her, and he slammed a fist into his palm and said softly, 'Musa.' Then he moved towards her, his eyes wild with fury, 'That settles it. That settles it. That settles it.' Three times.

'Jakpa,' Akosua asked. 'Why must you avenge his brother's death?'

'His brother did not die, Akosua. I am he.'

She looked as if she didn't understand.

He repeated, 'I am his brother, Akosua, whom he left to his fate. Now I have returned, and my heart is longing for vengeance.'

'Jakpa!' The word came out in a hoarse whisper. Her eyes were open wide, as if he had been a ghost returning from the dead.

'I loved my brother, Akosua,' he said. 'I loved him to the point of foolishness. He was the most handsome youth of Kumbili, and I felt proud when all the girls cast him looks, even as the women of Kumasi look at him today with desire. He was brave and strong. I remember well how even the oldest hunters liked his company and always invited him to come along. He was the best Kokoa wrestler in the whole neighbourhood for many miles around. At twenty-one years he beat the older, much more experienced champion, and was never defeated till he ran away with her who is now no more. He taught me to shoot the bow and to fight with both sword and spear. I worshipped him, Akosua.'

He waited, as if allowing her time to cut in to ask questions, but Akosua stood looking at him and did not utter a word.

63

He continued, 'I should not have loved him so much, Akosua, but I was blind. I saw only his good side. Maybe it is because of our father. He made us feel strangers all the time in Kumbili with his constant reminders of our people in Gonja. The result was that we three felt strong bonds towards one another. When Baba died, I was broken. For many weeks I ate poorly, till long after the funeral. My brother had his woman to confide his sorrow in, but I had nobody. My mother had died before my father, and between us and Baba's other wives there existed few bonds of affection – they were jealous that we were the favourites of Baba. Akosua, I thought I had come to the biggest hurdle in my life, but I didn't know what was to follow. Just when I was overcoming the heavy sorrow of my father's death, just a few months after the final funeral rites, my brother told me of his love for Mbinge, and together we approached her father, the village headman. But he turned down our offer saying that the girl was already promised to someone. My brother got ill, Akosua, and I was afraid he would die and I would be alone in the world. I loved my father, my sister, but I think even more than him I loved my handsome, courageous brother. I knew the strong stubborn love he had for the girl, and I knew him well enough to know that only she could make him well again. So I begged – yes, I begged him – to get well so that we could abduct the girl together. Has he told of the part I played in her abduction?'

She nodded. 'How did you escape, Jakpa?' she asked. 'He told how you rode with him to the river Sisili, and how you were captured. What happened to you? Why are you not dead?'

'Why am I not dead?' he repeated, as if amused by the question. 'It is something I have often asked myself. I have suffered because of my foolish love for Seku the ungrateful, Seku the selfish. I lay there in the mud at the riverside, too weak to stand, disbelieving that he whom I had loved and worshipped so truly could leave me to my fate. Three arrows had hit me – in the back, arm and left calf. The Mossi were furious. The leading riders threw themselves down from their charging horses to be the first to reach me. The others rode a few strides into the river, but the water was too deep, and the crocodiles of the river seemed to see now that something was happening. Several of them would have ridden along the banks following the dug-out canoe, but the leader of the band, one of Mbinge's own brothers but from another mother, told them to return because of fear of entering Dagomba territory. They shouted threats across, and they picked me up and slapped and beat me. They held me up so that my brother could see I was alive, but he paddled on. They waited there with me till he was out of sight, and I think they would have killed me had it not been for Mbinge's brother. The men gave loud cries of anguish as the canoe disappeared round the bend, and several of them drew their daggers to finish me off, but Mbinge's brother cried out telling them that maybe Seku would return for me, so that they could catch him then. The men reluctantly sheathed their weapons, and they put me on a horse and headed for home. I lost my senses on the way. When I came to, I was lying in my room. A fetish priest had cut out the arrow-heads and I was heavily bandaged. He told me that the chief knew the part I had played in abducting his daughter and that he was enraged. But he had great respect for my father and would not mistreat me if my brother returned with the girl. Akosua my sister, they would have preferred not to harm me. Mbinge was their pride, and they had big plans for her. They were hopeful my brother's love for me and his conscience would bring him back, and I also thought and prayed it would happen so. But the days passed and turned into weeks, and I could feel increasing hate for me.

'Finally after eight weeks the chief himself came to see me. By this time I could stand and walk a little. He was angry and afraid for his daughter, and he told me that I had three days to get well. If at the end of that time his daughter was still not there, then I would be chained day and night at a stake in the middle of the village. If after two weeks they still hadn't returned, I would be killed. My heart was heavy and I was afraid, but so long as a man has life in him, he believes in survival. Even when after three days the chief's guards came to lead me to the stake, I still hoped they would come. I was chained up in the middle of the village. All the people came to watch, the men angry and scowling, the women with pity on their silent faces. I suffered terribly. My arms and legs were chained behind my back, and I was fed like a baby by one old woman twice a day. The flies were bothersome – I couldn't swat at them, and in the end I just gave up shaking my head to drive them off. The sun was hot, my tongue dry, and I itched in many parts of the body from the dust in the air, but I couldn't scratch myself. At night it got cool, then cold and windy, and I froze. After three days of suffering like this I could bear no more, and I begged them to kill me and end my suffering. They only laughed. They asked me to tell them where my brother was headed, but I didn't know, and they didn't believe me. I was almost relieved when the chief came to me one morning and said he had discussed the matter with the village elders, and that I was to be stoned to death. It is a strange thing, Akosua, but I think death is not so unbearable as men think. True, I didn't die that day – else I wouldn't be here now – but I think I reached the very threshold of the doors of death. The whole village, including even children, took part. Some had been my friends, but now they were afraid. The chief had sent word to the prince in Wagadugu, Mbinge's fiancée, and they feared the anger of the man, so all who were innocent of the crime took part in my stoning. I looked up at them standing before me, with baskets of stones and rocks before them. The oldest villager stepped forward, staggering under the weight of a large rock. He spoke loudly for all to hear, telling of my crime, and asking my father's forgiveness, but justice was justice. He threw the rock with surprising force and it hit me on the thigh. Then followed the hail. I cried and twisted with pain, but the chains held me up, unprotected. Then a strange thing happened to my senses, Akosua. Suddenly I realised that I felt no pain, no fear. It was as if it was all a dream. I saw my arms pulling at the chains, and it seemed to be somebody else's, because the hands were tugging desperately, yet my mind was calm and peaceful. I do not know to this day if Allah took pity on me and relieved me of feeling any pain, or if it is His way of making death come more easily to His creatures. Maybe it is His method to ensure that the antelope attacked by the lion does not die painfully, but calmly, almost blissfully. When I see a chicken being beheaded nowadays, I am filled with wonder, because I remember my experience that day, and I know that despite its fluttering, in reality shock has dulled all feelings, and the bird does not suffer.

'I do not remember how I collapsed. It gradually got darker and darker, and I fell into a dreamless sleep of darkness. After what seemed an eternity I woke up. It was night, but I was so sure I was dead that I thought it was the land of the dead. The air was deadly calm, I could hear no beastly cries. I wondered if I was in heaven, for all was so quiet, but no prophets came to welcome me, and I thought, Jakpa, you committed a beastly sin. The people who sheltered your beloved father and yourself, the people who have given you a home, you have cheated them. Where else can you be but in the other place where sinners go? I made an attempt to rise. The pain shot through my back and I lay down again with a hollow cry, hollow even to my ears. It was then that I realised I was lying on a mat, wet and sticky with my own blood. I carefully reached out an arm, and I touched some grass. So, I thought, Satan also grows grass in his home! I wondered where the great fire was.'

'After the third or fourth attempt, I succeeded in rising onto rubbery legs. I touched my body carefully, but my hands were shaking so much that I couldn't really ascertain well where my body was most swollen. Suddenly I saw two shadowy forms watching me intently, and my heart jumped and I nearly collapsed again. The demons had come to fetch me to the fires of Hell! I started backing away, terrified, but they didn't follow, just stood there watching. I fell on my knees and began praying aloud to Allah, reciting all the verses I loved dearly.

'The two forms came up to me slowly. I bowed down my head and continued praying, louder. Still they watched me, and finally I just couldn't go on praying aloud, because I felt so weak and tired. However, I mentally recited the prayers.

'One of them finally spoke. "Do not fear, Jakpa," he said. "We have not come to hurt you."

'At the sound of the voice I looked up hopefully. But it couldn't be! Musa was not dead, he had even partaken in my stoning. What was he doing in Hell?

' "Here is water," Musa repeated, offering a calabash.

'I drank. Then I looked again at the two. Musa I had recognised from his voice, but the other one remained a mystery. Musa was dressed in a white smock, like men generally wore, but the other person was obviously a woman. She also had a white cloth round her body from the knees to below the breasts. On the head was a white head scarf. Her face was as black as the darkness, and it was impossible to see her features.

'Musa spoke again. "We are happy you have survived, Jakpa. But you must escape." '

' "Then I still live?" I asked disbelievingly.

'He assured me that I was still alive. Then he handed out a long spear saying, "Here, take it. You will need it to remind you that you still live, and later, it will provide you with food and protection."

'I took the spear, felt its hardness, then rammed it into the ground with all the feeble force I could muster. Slowly it dawned on me that I hadn't died, but was much alive. And I didn't know whether to be happy or sad, because now I had no home, and I was all alone in the world.

'Musa explained that I had been stoned to unconsciousness, then the villagers had brought my still body to a clearing far away from any human dwelling and left me on a mat as an offering to the hyenas. Because of my crime there would be no honourable burial. The villagers had not killed me outright, but had left that to the hyenas.

'The hyenas! I hadn't thought of them. Akosua, my sister, the hyena has the most powerful jaws of any living creature. The bones that defy a lion, they make no problem for the hyena, which joyfully cracks the leg bones of dead elephants. Though it enjoys carrion, it hunts weak creatures in packs. A healthy armed man need not fear these beasts even if they are in large packs – they simply run away when he waves his arms and shouts. But it is another story if he is sick or weak, or if he is bleeding. Even the bravest hunters dare not sleep without fires to scare away the cowardly, strong-jawed monsters. I do not know if you of the forests have hyenas, or if they are as big as those in my area, but over there they are feared and hated terribly.

'Musa said, "You have been here for several hours since morning. If the beasts have not yet attacked you, then you owe it to this lady, who came to me in my hut soon after your body had been carried away. She suggested that we save you."

'I looked at the lady. She came closer, and then I suddenly recognised her. I was filled with shame, and I went on my knees before her. It was Mbinge's mother, the chief's own wife. I had stolen her daughter away, yet she had come to save me, risking the anger of even her husband. I begged her to forgive me.

'"Do not grieve," said this kind lady. "I wish to tell you that I forgive you what you have done me and my husband. My husband is depressed – because of his ambitions, but I am sad because I have lost a daughter. You did what you did because you loved your brother. I understand love, for I am a woman. You have been punished enough. I respected your Moslem father very much. He tilled the land the chief my husband gave him industriously, and he did not spend all his wealth alone, but shared it well with others less fortunate than he. Because of him I have come to save you. Take the spear Musa has offered you and run. Do not fear for us. We have brought a dead gorilla which Musa trapped two days ago. The remains which the hyenas will leave won't be much, but it will convince the men when they check up tomorrow that the blood and bits of bones are yours."

'Musa helped me get onto my feet. He asked me to forgive him two things: first, he had given the chief the clue to catch us, and secondly he had partaken in my stoning. It wasn't difficult for me to forgive him these things. In the first place he had confessed only after being severely beaten, and even as I spoke with him in the darkness I saw or imagined his scars. Secondly, he had to partake in my stoning as everybody else, otherwise he would probably have joined me at the

68

stakes, for some of the men were still angry that he had held onto his secret and had not confessed willingly. Thirdly, how can a man just being saved hold grudges against his Messiah? I told him he was my closest friend, and that I would remember him well. I also thanked him for trying to keep quiet what I had once told him, long before my brother fell in love, about what I believed to be the best way to escape from Mossi to Dagomba.

'I thanked them very much, and then as I turned to leave I stepped on a soft, cool body and the cry rose to my lips. Musa told me it was the body of the gorilla, which he had transported to the spot with the help of a horse. He had skinned it so that the chief's men wouldn't see that it had been a gorilla, and perhaps he would sell the skin later for a good price.

'I walked all night in a direction which led to I know not where. In the early morning I lit a fire and collapsed beside it. A small pack of hyenas had followed me. When I woke up at midday, they had been joined by vultures, all sitting in a circle watching me patiently. I felt hungry, and I got up to look for some wild roots and berries. I threw stones at the scavengers, but they only went back a few steps and did not run away. Five days passed, and I grew weaker and weaker. The hyenas got impatient. One of them suddenly ran at me, but Allah , protected me, and I rammed my spear down its throat. The other hyenas became very excited at the smell of blood. To prevent them attacking me, I cut off the head with the cutting edge of the spear and threw it to them. Then I prepared a small fire and ate some meat for the first time in many days. Don't pull faces, Akosua, my sister. Hyena flesh is surprisingly tender and succulent. I roasted the thighs and liver of the scavenger and tied them to my waist for future meals.

'After some ten or fourteen days – I know not exactly – I was picked up by some Dagomba hunters. By this time I was so weak and hungry that I had nearly given up all hope. The hyena meat was long finished, and I was simply starving. The number of hyenas had greatly increased, as had that of the vultures. I stumbled, and the hyenas began to growl and to give their barks of laughter. Suddenly I heard different barks from quite nearby, then three tall Fulani dogs came into view. You of Asante do not know these fine, slender dogs. In the plains, they are used to track down lions, so great is their courage. The cowardly hyenas scattered out of their way and they stood at my side barking joyfully. The three Dagomba riders came and helped me onto a horse, and I collapsed before I could thank them properly. They took me to their tiny hamlet of five houses, and I was nursed for several weeks. They were kind to me, but I noticed that the women felt pity for me. At first I thought it was because of how ill I was, but when I got better and even went farming with them, the looks persisted. Finally I asked one woman to explain, but she refused, and I became more and more confused and afraid. I went to see the oldest of the three hunters who had saved my life with the intention of thanking him and asking for leave to continue with my journey, but he wouldn't hear of it. So I stayed on and went farming with the women and some of the men.

'I noticed that two of the men always carried spears, and after I had told the hunter I wanted to leave, I saw why. They watched me closely, and it was obvious that they were guarding against my escape. Some three or four months after I had come to the village, everything became fully clear. The two guards refused to allow me to join those going to farm, and at about midday a strange procession of people came to the village. They were some of the slave collectors of the Ya Na going round all Dagomba for the "contributions". There were about thirty slaves in chains: men, a few women and even two children. My villagers were happy they had found me, else they would have had to give up one of their number to these men. I was taken and chained at the rear of the chain-gang, and before we started off again, I looked hard at the villagers whom I had thanked for saving my life. They looked away, ashamed. We marched for four days before reaching Yendi, the capital. Each time we reached a hamlet on the way, we stopped to collect more slaves, till by the time we were in Yendi there were over a hundred of us. We were camped in an open space outside the town, where several hundred other slaves were already waiting.

'Early the next morning, the Asante came to inspect us. We were ordered to stand up, stark naked, for them. They felt our muscles, looked at the eyeballs, opened the mouths for a look, and one of them lifted my manhood with a stick and said something, whereupon his companions laughed. They led the weaker specimens aside and the Dagombas promised to replace them. On the fourth day after our arrival in Yendi the Asante were ready to leave, and we were introduced to the style under which we would be taken to the south. The Asante guards were fewer by far than the Dagomba guards had been but they were more efficient. Every two male slaves had a heavy plank of wood borne on the shoulders, with notches for the heads, these notches being padlocked at the ends so that it was impossible to get rid of the logs. Our hands were chained behind the back and our legs were loosely chained so that we couldn't take long strides. The women and children were spared the heavy logs, but they too bore chains on the arms and legs, and all of us were chained in long continuous rows. We kept on the chains at all times, except during meal times when the arms were unchained, and at night, when the logs were removed. I assure you, my sister, it was an unforgettable experience.

'On our way to Yendi only one slave committed suicide by the incredible feat of holding his breath, but many more died on the way between Yendi and Kumasi. At first the guards allowed us to bathe our stinking bodies whenever we came to a stream, but seven slaves drowned themselves, and this privilege was lost. The flies were bothersome and when we relieved ourselves, we couldn't clean our anuses, and so each slave had his special colony of flies there, and it was only after several of us got ill that they allowed us to clean our bodies again in water. There was a small rebellion. Four slaves seized some guards as their arms were untied for the meal, and other guards panicked and fired into the air, intending to scare the rebels into submissiveness. But the shots frightened all the slaves into a stampede, and though none of us got far, by the time order had been restored, the slaves had strangled their victims to death. The guards murdered the four rebels by sepo, and all of us were severely whipped. But I think you know the rest of my story, sister, so I shall not continue any further. I am sure your uncle Nana Amoaten has told you how he came to calm the guards and led us to Kumasi under far better conditions, and how he was awarded two slaves for his troubles and he chose me. This is the story of my coming to Kumasi. It is not a nice story, but it is the truth.'

Jakpa sat down on the stool he had first offered his listener. Akosua was silent and had nothing to say.

Jakpa said, 'You have asked me to explain why Seku Wattara must die. He deceived and betrayed me, and now he has killed my best friend who saved the life he rejected. In these hard times, people die for less. Do you see now why Seku must die?'

Akosua replied, 'Until this evening you did not know that Musa was dead. Would you have changed your mind if Seku had spared your friend?'

'No, my sister. My mind was already decided on his death.'

'You are hard, Jakpa.'

'I must be, sister. I've learnt that in this world we all stand alone. None really cares for another person.'

'He is your brother.'

'I am his brother as well, but he left me to die.'

Akosua hesitated a little before saying, 'You must hate my people.'

He looked at her and shook his head slowly. 'Perhaps I should. Your people have conquered mine, they have devastated my people and many others, and they have treated me as a slave. But my heart sees only one person at fault: Seku Wattara. Him I hate and him I must destroy.'

'My uncle was the man who led those who enslaved you.'

'I do not dislike him, Akosua. He was only obeying orders, and Allah knows he hated the cruelty of his helpers.'

'Think of your father, Jakpa. He wouldn't forgive you if you don't forgive your brother.'

'My sister, my brother betrayed my father also. My father was a great Moslem Imam who did all he could to make us follow in his steps. My brother not only stopped learning to read and write, he even refused to pray any longer to Allah. Worse even than that, he has now ruined the good memories the Mossi had of our father, whom they respected.'

'Think of the little child, Jakpa. It will have neither mother nor father if you should kill Seku.'

'I do think of it, Akosua. I shall bring it up as my own. Seku does not deserve a son.'

'Hear me, Jakpa,' Akosua pleaded desperately, 'I am an orphan as well. My uncle is good to me, but I cannot help wishing my parents were still alive and with me. Are you blind? Can't you see the pain you will cause the child who will surely find out that it was you who made him an orphan?'

'If he finds out,' Jakpa replied carelessly, 'he can kill me. I am tired of this world anyway. Perhaps you will look after the child for both of us. The abrafo will gladly butcher me if I should dare attack the hero of the Gyaaman war.'

Akosua said angrily, 'You are mad, mad, mad! He is by far your superior in strength. Why do you want to commit suicide like this? Did you want the dead woman so much?'

He got up and grabbed her left wrist in a fierce hold so that she winced with the pain. 'I never felt love for her,' he said. 'But her mother saved my life. I did think she was a good woman, and it is partly because of her that I have not been able to make final preparations to kill him until this time. But now she is gone, and he will soon follow.'

He let go, and she sat down on the stool and caressed her wrist soothingly. Jakpa towered over her, then his anger burned to shame, and he wanted to say something comforting. Her shoulders were heaving slightly, almost unnoticeably, and he saw that she was weeping. He went to put an arm round her shoulders, but she shook him off, and he stood watching silently till she could shed no more tears. She wiped her eyes with the ends of her cloth, and said quietly:

'It is sad to be a woman, Jakpa. We have feelings even we ourselves do not understand. Sometimes, I wish I had been a man, because men seem so much more independent. I felt like a traitor at the funeral, because I knew I went there because of someone, and now, so soon after the funeral, here I am again with that someone. A man can love seven wives at the same time, but a woman's heart is always for one man, even if he doesn't deserve it. When a man loses a wife, unless he is a man of iron discipline like Seku, it is no problem finding another to replace her. But a woman forced into marrying another man will always treasure the memory of the one she really loves. Go and die, Jakpa. I cannot stop you from killing yourself.'

Jakpa went and put a hand on her shoulder and with the other hand he forced her to face him. 'Akosua,' he said gently, 'I treasure the kind affections you have for me. It is something I didn't suspect was there. I wish I could promise something in return, but I made my vow and for a man, honour and integrity come before all else, even love.'

She got up from her stool and said, 'I am going, Jakpa. But before I go, I must have this promise: whatever you do, wait till after the forty days.'

'Forty days?'

'Yes. There will be the final funeral rites for the lady on the fortieth day after the death. Promise to allow Seku to take part in these rites.'

Jakpa looked at her a long moment then said, 'Very well. But only because of you.'

He accompanied her to the front gates of the palace. Some of the guards looked at them curiously, but neither cared about it. Jakpa stood watching her till she went round a side street, then he decided himself to go for a walk in the opposite direction. Akosua went to her stall in the market to check the sales made by the maids. They were eager to chat and pressed her for information concerning the burial, but she showed no interest and they gave up. She thought all afternoon but she couldn't see any possibilities of stopping Jakpa from killing his brother after the fortieth-day funeral rites.

73

6

Otumfuor the Asantehene was very sick. For many weeks he had made no public appearance, and the faces of the fetish priests and attendants were grim. Few people loitered in the vicinity of the palace, and for good reason. For when the Otumfuor died, no immediate announcement was made till all the important chiefs had been summoned by the Bantamahene, and even then the news would be kept silent till the abrafo had captured a few victims to serve the deceased monarch in the land of the dead. The announcement of the death was accompanied by a curfew, and any one breaking this curfew was destined to serve in the land of the dead as well if caught.

Otumfuor Opoku II had not actively performed his duties as Asantehene for many weeks. The Bantamahene now took his place in court cases, and at one Adae he made the offerings in place of the king, who could not even sit up in bed. That was during a Wednesday Wukudae, and three weeks later, as the time approached for a Sunday Kwasidae, there was a great public outcry to see the king and to know if he was still alive or not. Maalam Fuseini paid an unexpected call on Jakpa and said that he had been asked by the Gyaasehene to pray for the king's health. Perhaps Allah would grant them what the gods of Asante could not give. Jakpa fetched some goat skins, and the two Moslems prayed for many hours in Jakpa's little courtyard. Several of the eunuchs looked on curiously.

On the Saturday evening preceding the Sunday of the Adae festival, there was continuous drumming before the palace till just before dawn. A crowd gathered before the gates, for what the drummers were saying was that the king was well and would play his part in the Kwasidae. The women sang till sunrise, and the combined noise of their singing and the drums kept Jakpa awake all night.

He went to watch the celebrations. As was usual during such activities, a large crowd had gathered to watch the public ceremony, but the king and his attendants were late in coming. Kofi, Jakpa's servant, remarked that perhaps his illness had returned, but Jakpa was more optimistic. He knew that there was a special rite in the palace which only the king and a few attendants performed. There was a special house in the centre of the palace where the favourite stools of the deceased royal ancestors were kept. The Golden Stool of Asante was also kept there, and the ancestral stools were blackened with sacrificial blood. This place was considered the home of the ancestral ghosts or spirits, and they were more likely to be found there than elsewhere. The king, acting as a common servant (for what is he after all but the first servant of the ancestors?) would himself dish out food, meat and drink for the spirits, barefooted and with bare shoulders.

Jakpa's guess turned out to be right, because after some time the king's retinue made its appearance. Since the Adae festival was celebrated separately in each state every three weeks, none of the state Amanhene was present; only the king's own chiefs of Kumasi came. Jakpa took a good long look at Opoku II. He sat calmly in his palanquin and he looked quite well from far away, but when he passed closely by, he looked hollow-eyed and weak, and his waving actions seemed to require great efforts from him. All the time the palace musicians recited important happenings in the history of the nation in songs. As the king stepped from the palanquin to get seated he stumbled, and two of his chiefs hastened to give a hand. The people held their breath, for if he had fallen many sacrifices would have been needed to avert a calamity. It was taboo for any part of the king's person to touch the bare soil during a public ceremony.

Despite the king's public appearance, his illness was not better. It had required a great effort on his part to rise and perform before his people, and in the following days and weeks he was confined to his chambers. The Bantamahene of Kumasi took over the administration, presiding over court cases and receiving visitors on behalf of the king. A great many fetish priests were consulted for cures, and occasionally Maalam Fuseini was asked to pray by the king's bedside. He told Jakpa that the king's situation was very critical.

In the midst of all these troubles Jakpa's servant Kofi decided to take a wife, and he chose the sister of one of the palace eunuchs. Jakpa was annoyed at first, as he had other problems on his mind, and didn't want to be distracted by bride-prices and visits to his servant's future in-laws, but as the arrangements and talks continued into weeks he had to admit that the whole affair did help to take his mind off Seku Wattara, at least for the six weeks he had promised Akosua.

Finally, about a week after Kofi's marriage, the fortieth-day funeral

75

celebrations for Mbinge were held. Akosua came the day before to inform Jakpa, and she promised to call on him again on the morning after the rites. It was clear that her intentions were to make yet another plea to detain him, and since he wanted to avoid another quarrel with her, he decided to go to Seku's house on the night of the ceremony. He had a bath and said a long prayer at dusk, and when Kofi brought him supper he told him to take it away.

He walked slowly towards Aboabo. The moon was so bright that he cast a clear shadow, and it was easy to see the way ahead. He was greeted respectfully by many passers-by, and he replied politely with a little bow. In Aboabo he asked to be shown the house, and an old man led him there personally. Jakpa thanked him as he left him at the doorsteps, and he knocked at the wooden door.

It was opened by a servant. He was in mourning cloths and he appeared very tired. He did not ask Jakpa who he was or what he wanted, but led him towards Seku's private room and knocked. The house was quite empty of people, as the mourners had all left for their homes, and it had a gloomy and sad atmosphere surrounding it.

A short, stout man opened the door slightly and said to the servant, 'Dwomo, Opanin Seku is tired. Don't let in any more guests.' Then he saw Jakpa and said, 'Ah, Kramo, forgive me. I didn't see you. This is a rare honour. You will be the first Kramo to be coming to offer condolence. My name is Ntiamoah.'

Jakpa shook his hand and said, 'Can I see him?'

Ntiamoah did not seem to like the proposal. He replied, 'You are an honourable man, Kramo, but he is tired. We haven't eaten all day, and we have sung, prayed and made offerings at the graveyard. The sorrow added to all this makes it unwise for me to lead you to see him, for he is truly weak and needs rest.'

Jakpa persisted, 'It is important.'

'I assure you, Kramo, it is not his will that you be sent away like this, but he is ill, and we are both his friends, and know it would be better not to disturb him.'

Jakpa repeated, 'It is important.'

Ntiamoah now looked squarely at him and said, 'You force me to say the truth. He is sick and as drunk as a fish. He has become the worst drunkard I know of in this town. I managed to force him to leave the drink alone for today, but he is back at it now, and I can't stop him.'

'I have come to cure him of this habit,' Jakpa said. Ntiamoah didn't seem convinced, so he added, 'Tell him Jakpa is here.'

The name didn't seem to have any effect on Ntiamoah. But he relented a little bit and said, 'Since you insist, Kramo, come in, but only for a few moments.'

He opened the door and they went in.

Seku was half-sitting, half lying on a straw mattress propped up on a stool. He was naked but for some cotton trousers, and he was sipping palm wine from a calabash. Beside him was a number of empty small pots of the alcohol, with two or three full pots nearby. Much of the drink had spilled over his chest and on the floor, and the room stank. It was one big mess: stools in disorder, cloths everywhere on the floor. He didn't pay attention as the door was opened and closed.

Ntiamoah went up to him and said, 'Seku, there is one more visitor.'

To Jakpa's surprise Seku got up automatically, and he stood swaying and said something about forgiving him for his sad state, but Jakpa didn't understand it fully. Seku sat down again. Jakpa went closer so that the light was well reflected on his face, then he stood waiting for the effect. Seku looked up again to address his guest, then the words seemed to stick in his throat and his eyes opened wide. Jakpa remained very still. Seku stared for several moments, he looked away, then he looked again and again. He suddenly seemed very sober. He grabbed Ntiamoah's arm and said, 'Yaw my brother, tell me what you see before us. I think my sight is impaired.'

Ntiamoah looked and saw only Jakpa. He replied, 'I shall call the herbalists tomorrow, Seku. They will cure your eyes.'

Seku shook his head. 'The guest you have brought me – describe him well. Do I see what you see?'

Ntiamoah looked and said, 'It is only a Kramo, Seku...'

'Then it is true, it is true!' The cry broke from Seku's lips. He stood up and, still looking at Jakpa he took his friend's arm and said, 'Yaw, he has returned, he has returned to me!'

Again Ntiamoah looked at Jakpa and said, 'Who, Seku? Who has returned?'

'My brother, Yaw, my brother Jakpa. Are you blind? I have a guest. A very special guest. We must prepare the place for him. I shall call the servants.'

He danced excitedly up and down, but he appeared too scared to pass his guest at the door to call the servants.

Ntiamoah asked, 'Who are you, silent Kramo? Speak, if you are a living man like we are.'

Jakpa made no answer, and Seku pulled back his friend. 'Let him be,

Yaw. He is my brother, son of my father and my mother. I must go before him, I must tell him of what has happened to me. She has left me, Jakpa,' he addressed him, 'we finished the final burial rites today. My heart had a great emptiness, but now that I have seen you I know you will guide her there in the new world. I know you have come to tell me she is fine. But you must protect our son too, for she left me a son, a small handsome boy. I must show him to you. How is Baba, my brother? How is our mother? Did they send you to tell me all is right again? I have suffered, brother, and it seems I can't bear any more now that Mbinge too has left me. I am all alone, and I am afraid.'

He went closer and said, 'I must touch you, Jakpa. I must feel those muscles I helped develop, for you were a weak child till I taught you how to fight to defend yourself. Let me touch you, let me touch you.' Each time he made this petition he inched forward, then he went on his knees before his brother and wept into the lower folds of his white smock.

Jakpa stepped back abruptly, so that Seku had to put out an elbow to prevent his head hitting the floor, then he spoke for the first time, 'This is no ghost who addresses you, Seku Wattara. This is a man of flesh and blood. I did not die when you left me, you coward, but I have been allowed to live and to find your whereabouts. Truly, Allah is just.'

Ntiamoah helped Seku onto his feet, and they both stood watching Jakpa. Jakpa put his hand into the flames of the torch, and waited till it burned him enough for a cry to come to his lips, then he showed his scorched finger nails. Seku did not immediately believe, but Ntiamoah said, more confidently, 'Kramo, you have given us a fright. We are glad you are a man like we, and that you know my friend personally. Sit down and let us talk.'

Jakpa did not sit. 'I have only little to say. This man Wattara betrayed me, and I am after his blood. He need mourn no longer, for he will soon join his wife in the land of the dead.'

Ntiamoah spoke soothingly, 'You say shocking things, Kramo. First of all, there are two of us, and secondly, I let you in, so you will have to kill me first to get at him.'

Jakpa bowed slightly, 'As you wish. But I have not come to kill today. Let Seku Wattara rest and be prepared for when I shall come. He must get a fair chance, for after all, he is my full brother.'

Ntiamoah shook his head. 'You are a fool, Kramo. What will prevent us from sending assassins to waylay you? Now is your chance. You will never get it again.'

But Jakpa would not be drawn into a fight at that moment. His reply was short: 'I think not.' Then he turned to go out. Even as he opened the door a hoarse voice called out the single word: 'Jakpa.'

He turned to face his brother. Seku was looking desperately at him, as if torn in a deep inner struggle. He asked, 'Is it true that you live?'

Jakpa walked forward for him to feel his clothes and body. He remained hard and impassive till Seku had finished touching him, and stood looking at the floor. Then he asked, 'Do you believe now, son of my father?'

Seku nodded slowly, still looking at the floor, 'Yes, I do.'

Jakpa said, 'Prepare, Wattara. I have had two knives prepared for us. I have used the emblem of Nyame, for we both work now for the same master, the Asantehene.'

Seku looked up suddenly, 'Then you are the Jakpa I had heard of. My wife had a friend, Akosua Kyem, niece of Nana Amoaten. She told us that one of the new palace secretaries was a Gonja called Jakpa who used to live with them.'

'Yes, I am the same. Why did you not check up?'

Seku shook his head. 'We were convinced my brother was dead, and that this one was only his name-sake. I beg of you, Jakpa, I thought, I thought —' He stopped.

Jakpa smiled grimly. 'You thought I was dead, Wattara, because you left me to die. You used me to get what you wanted, then you left me for the hyenas.'

'I had no choice, Jakpa. I had to think of Mbinge as well, not only you.'

'I would have given my life for you, Seku. You had other priorities in mind. My life is not worth saving, to you.'

Seku was silent for some time, then he said, 'Brother of mine, tell me what happened. In Gyaaman I was told that you had been stoned to death.'

'Yes, I was stoned, and my unconscious body left in the plain as an offering for the hyenas. Musa, whom you killed came to save my life.'

Seku looked sharply at his brother. 'Musa told me you were dead and that I would also die soon. He admitted that it was he who had betrayed us, and since he did not show respect when mentioning your death, I slew him. Why did he not tell me the truth?'

'Why should he, proud Seku? He was my friend, and he hated you for betraying me. Why should he tell you I had survived when you had rejected me?'

'He betrayed you too, Jakpa.'

'But only under torture, and anyway, he made up for it. Your betrayal was of the worst kind, for I had loved and respected you greatly.'

Seku asked, 'How did you come to Kumasi?'

Jakpa smiled. 'As a slave, brother of mine. I was captured in Dagomba and turned over to the Kumasi slave collectors when they came to Yendi. I was dragged completely naked through the grasslands and forests with heavy logs on my shoulders. I was fortunate not to complete the journey down to the coast for the white men to ship to their land across the Great Sea. I was chosen to be a personal servant in the good Nana Amoaten's home till, Allah being so good, the good Imam at the palace came to call me to help him. I have suffered because of you, brother Seku, and the time is ripe for a much-needed revenge.'

'I have a son now, Jakpa.'

'So I have heard. Unfortunate baby, so he will see life without either parent. Do not use your son as an excuse, Seku, coward. You betrayed your own father easily enough, and I know you would betray your son too if it served your purpose. I shall ask someone to look after him.'

'I understand, Jakpa,' said Seku after a thoughtful pause. 'I understand your feelings. I am prepared to die for the wrong I did.'

'Seku!' Ntiamoah cut in sharply. 'Let me deal with this man who threatens you —'

'No, my brother Yaw,' Seku shook his head. 'Promise me this – that you will leave him alone in peace. His cause is just.'

He looked fixedly at Ntiamoah till he reluctantly nodded without speaking. They both waited for Jakpa to say something, and after a few silent moments he said:

'Prepare, Wattara. I go now, but within ten days you will hear from me again. When we next meet, only one of us will return alive.'

With that he turned and left.

Seku sat down shakily on a stool. He tried to detain Ntiamoah as he started for the door, but his friend shook his head to show that he was not thinking of violence, then he hurried out after Jakpa. He caught up with him just outside the main entrance of the house, and called, 'Kramo!'

Jakpa faced him.

'Your brother is a good man, Kramo. He is well-respected in Kumasi. Think it over, because the elders will be angry if you should strike him.'

80

'But I shall.'

Ntiamoah saw that he was very determined, so he decided it would be foolish to argue further. He said, 'As you wish. But I warn you, if Seku dies, I shall kill you with my own hands. He is the finest man I have ever met.'

With that he turned and went back to the house. Jakpa walked home without a backward glance.

A few days later Jakpa called on Maalam Fuseini. The Imam was in the process of leaving his house, and when he saw Jakpa he said, 'My son, I was just coming to see you.'

He led him into his room. He asked after his health, then after offering kola he lowered his voice and said in Arabic, 'One must be careful in Kumasi now. The king died last night in his sleep. I was there when it happened. This is a secret, Jakpa – do not tell anyone. When the elders want to announce it they shall do so. Restrict the freedom of your servant till it becomes public knowledge, then he himself will understand why he must stay home.' It is customary for the executioners to capture victims to serve the king in the land of the dead.

Jakpa thanked him for the news, and promised to follow the advice.

'The Mamponghene has been sent for,' Maalam Fuseini went on. 'He shall assume command of the nation till after the burial and succession have taken place. The news will be publicly announced after he and other important chiefs have arrived in the capital.'

'There will be many deaths, then?' Jakpa asked.

'I do not know. Certainly a few people must accompany the king, but Opoku ruled for only a short insignificant time. Keep your eyes and ears open, for many interesting things will happen. First of all, only a few important people will be allowed to see the body. The whole town will be full of lamentations, for all must weep at the Great Otumfuor's "journey somewhere". Anybody not wearing funeral cloths in public can be seized and butchered by the abrafo.'

'And the burial?'

'That will also be done in secrecy. The body will be sent to the great Mausoleum in Bantama. This is a big building with many chambers. The remains of Asante kings are kept there, a body in a chamber, and when the flesh has rotted away, the bones are bound together with golden wires.'

Jakpa said, 'There will be trouble. Osei Kwame still lives.'

Maalam Fuseini shook his head. 'Osei Kwame will never be king again. He is extremely unpopular among the elders of Asante, and only his distant Moslem subjects like him, but they have no power. What is more I hear that he himself is rather ill and may die soon. This is how the new Asantehene will be elected. The Kontihene of Kumasi, the Bantamahene, will ask the Gyaasehene to approach the queen-mother for a candidate. The Gyaasehene in turn will summon all Kumasi chiefs, war captains and elders, and they will choose a delegation to approach the queen-mother formally. Kingship in Asante is vested in a single segment of the Oyoko matri-clan. Only those who claim descendance through a woman of this special family have a right to contest for the highest post in the land. The queen-mother will consult the members of this family, and then she will present a candidate for the Kumasi chiefs. If the chiefs reject her candidate, she may choose twice again, but after her third candidate has been rejected, the chiefs will choose their own man. Note that only the Kumasi chiefs elect the Asantehene, who is first chief of the capital, then also king of all Asante. The Amanhene have no official say in these elections, but they publicly back candidates, and the queen-mother and the Kumasi chiefs have to give due consideration to their preferences. Remember that Osei Kwame was deposed mainly by the Amanhene, who put pressure on the Kumasi elders.'

'This is a strange custom,' Jakpa remarked. 'I mean – that a woman should have so much say in the election of so powerful a man.'

'I agree, my son,' replied the Imam. 'But according to Asante tradition, in the old days the Asante were ruled by women. But a great number of wars came into their midst, and whenever the people approached her for advice and help during such a time, she always replied, "M'akyima", that is, that her period was on. In the end they agreed on a compromise: the people recognised her femininity, and asked that she give them a man to defend them. This is how the custom arose.'

'Who will be king, if it won't be Osei Kwame?'

'There are many capable men, Jakpa. But personally I suspect that Osei Tutu Kwame* will be elected. He is popular with the queen-mother, the chiefs and the Amanhene. I think he would make the best ruler for Asante.'

Jakpa had never met or heard of him. This was not unnatural, because the man had not enjoyed any special public privileges simply

* Later Osei Bonsu, the 'whale', conqueror of Fante.

82

for belonging to the family. He asked, 'Will he be a kind ruler? Will he give due consideration to his subjects far in the north or south?'

The Imam looked at Jakpa seriously. 'Yes, I believe so,' he said. 'I have spoken with him several times, and I believe that one of his first actions as king will be to pardon those Moslem rebels of Gyaaman who are under arrest. He is a tough man, but he has a heart as well. Now let us talk of our work, Jakpa. I shall need your help to put down many incidents, both as the elders of the palace wish it, and how perhaps I want it for my book.'

Jakpa asked, 'How are the plans for the school? You told me that you would consult Maalam Mumula and other Moslems to get it started. Did they agree to help you?'

The old man nodded, and the smile played on his lips. 'Yes, I am a very happy man now. Mumula is quite ready to work with me, and most of the other Moslems believe now that I am no traitor to the people of my belief. Mumula has even dismissed his two strong Dagomba men because they were too prone to violence, and he has become tired of paying compensation to those they beat up for coming too close to his home. One of their victims was the nephew of a senior obrani from the palace who asked the two men if they knew where he could get some grass-cutter meat, as it was not market-day. They were a little drunk, and took offence that the boy should suggest they were ordinary hunters of grass-cutters. The boy reported to his uncle when they beat him up, and he was so enraged that he nearly swore the Great Oath, which would have brought the chiefs into the case. Mumula had to promise to send away his men, and to pay a sizeable compensation.'

Jakpa asked again, 'Some time ago you told me that Maalam Fatai, who had sheltered Seku Wattara and who had shared ideas with you, had been mysteriously killed. Do you know now who killed him?'

The Imam shook his head. 'Siaka, the Fulani who killed Wattara's wife, has been executed by sepo. I asked the elders to ask him if he had killed Maalam Fatai, but he denied this. If he spoke the truth, then Maalam Fatai was murdered by fellow Moslems just as Tula, my assistant before you, was. But I do not worry about it, because now tempers have cooled, and moreover, neither Mumula nor any of the others now determined to work with me had anything to do with it, I am sure.'

Jakpa stood up and said he wanted to go and give instructions to Kofi to stay home, and the Imam said:

'It is good, but remember, don't tell him why. If the Gyaasehene finds out that I don't keep secrets, he may well look for another secretary. But before you go, let us arrange to meet again soon. This time Mumula will be present, and we shall discuss the school.'

Jakpa stared for a long moment at the floor then he straightened up and said, 'Forgive me, Maalam. You saved me from slavery, and you have been a father to me. It shames me to say this, but I want to stop working with you. It is the best way open for me.'

'Wha-what?' the old man stumbled over the words in his surprise. 'What do you mean, Jakpa? I don't think I understand.'

'Maalam, I have a duty to perform. In order that I perform it well, you must be free of me, because it could be a big burden for you.'

'Duty? What must you perform? Tell me.'

Jakpa was silent.

'My son,' the Imam asked earnestly, 'what have I done to you? Do I not give you enough gold dust as pocket money? Do I not show you a trust and affection I feel for no one else in this world? Or are you tired of living in a room in the palace? I have news for you: the elders have decided to build a home of your own in Zongo, not far from my own. I asked them for it. Is it land you want to farm, or money in order to start a trade?'

Jakpa said that it wasn't any of those things that was on his mind, then the Imam asked him:

'Then tell me the problem.'

Jakpa was silent.

The Imam was sad. He said, 'My son, I beg you to think again, whatever you have on your mind. Even if you don't need me, I need you. I need you for my school, for you are easily the best scholar I have met in this town, young as you are. I am old, and I shall soon die, and I would have liked one like you to continue with my work. Why must you leave at such a time? Why must you develop problems now? Tell me, is it the girl? I hear that a young Asante girl has been frequenting your rooms. Is she in the family way and you want to run away from it all? Remember, even Kofi the servant solved his problem by marrying his girl. Or do you not want her as your wife? Akosua Kyem is a beautiful girl, and I know her uncle as well as you do.'

Jakpa lowered his head in some embarrassment and said that it wasn't her. He said, 'I cannot tell you the full story, Maalam. But as the saying goes, blood is thicker than water. I have some family problems I must solve. I cannot tell you what it is because my mind is set on what

84

to do, and I cannot accept advice. Now I want to go, respectable Maalam. I know I am disappointing you, but I can't help myself.'

The Imam made no attempt to stop him, and he did not accompany him to the door. Jakpa paused in the doorway and looked back, but the old man stood stiff and silent staring away from him, so he drew the curtains gently and walked out.

He went to the market to warn Akosua about the Otumfuor's passing away. He thought the matter over, and though he hated to betray the Imam by repeating what he knew, he couldn't bear the thought of Akosua risking the danger of running into some abrafo. Sometimes she stayed in the market till very late, and he remembered how she had once encountered an obrani, who had fortunately turned out to be someone who knew her family: Kuntunkuni's son. But she might not be so lucky next time, and more, now it was the king himself who had died, not an ordinary member of the royal family.

She got up to welcome him, and he saw that for the first time since her friend's death she had put away her funeral cloths and was wearing a white cloth. Maame Ntosuor was there, as was one of the maids. The one nursing Seku's child had stayed at home with it. He greeted them, and they chatted. He asked about the health of Amoaten, his wives and children, and was told that they were all fine. Maame Ntosuor said:

'We are looking for a husband for Akosua. Many suitors are interested, but Nana Amoaten wants the very best for her.'

Jakpa looked at Akosua with some embarrassment: he had not yet kept his promise to dissuade her uncle from forcing her to marry old Kuntunkuni. She looked away from his eyes.

When he left the stall, she came to see him off. She would have turned back soon, but he said, 'Walk a bit with me, Akosua. I have something to tell you.'

When they were out of sight from the stall, he said in a lowered voice, 'Akosua, some important things are happening in this town. Promise me you will always leave market early, and that you will never wander out at night.'

She was afraid, 'What has happened?'

'I cannot tell you,' he replied, 'but trust me, and remember that I work in the palace.'

'The king,' she whispered, 'is he —'

'I cannot tell you,' he repeated. 'But promise to take care and to warn your family. But keep it a secret!'

She nodded, and thanked him for telling her. He wanted to leave now, but she suddenly grabbed his smock and stopped him. She asked:

'Are you going to see him?'

'The body? No, I won't be allowed to.'

'I meant your brother. When I came to see you the day after the funeral, you said you would go soon. Have you gone already?'

'No, not yet,' he lied for the second time to her. The first time he had lied was when he had told her he would go to Seku after she had come to him after the funeral day. In truth he had already seen his brother on the night of the funeral itself, the day before Akosua had visited him. 'But I shall,' he added.

'You will tell me before you do, won't you?' she asked.

He nodded, and she relaxed somewhat. She suddenly took his hand and pressed it hard, then she ran back towards her stall.

Two days later Jakpa polished his two daggers and put them into their bag. He donned his best white smock, and then told Kofi that he was going to 'visit', and told him that if he didn't return for supper, the servant should come with some of the eunuchs to fetch him at Aboabo. Kofi nodded obediently and went out to help one of his eunuch friends give food to the chickens. He didn't know what his master had in mind, of course, but it was none of his business so he didn't worry about it.

It was late afternoon. The sky was blood red in many parts, and all objects cast long shadows. There were several people on the road to Aboabo – farmers returning from their farms rather earlier than was normal. It seemed that news of the Otumfuor's passing away was not being so well kept as it should be, Jakpa thought.

He did not ask anybody to show him the house as he had already been there. Being the last house in Aboabo before the bushes, there would be few neighbours who would overhear the quarrel. There were few people around, and as he walked on the broad street, his footsteps made a noise that caused his heart to beat faster: crunch, crunch, crunch, crunch, crunch.

Two men were sitting some distance away from the main gateway, and when they saw him they moved slowly to block the gateway. It was the Bawa twins, tall and muscular, and they looked unfriendly. He came to a halt before them and said:

'Allow me to pass, my friends, I must see Opanin Seku.'

The elder twin, the wrestler, said with contempt in his voice,

'Opanin Seku meets only important officials, not pompous no-goods like you.'

'He is expecting me.'

They exchanged amused looks and laughed. 'Go and have a wash first, Kramo. The man dislikes evil smells,' said the older twin.

Jakpa swallowed his anger and said, 'Allow me to pass, my friends. I have no wish to harm you.'

'Harm us?' said the older twin. He exchanged looks with his brother and both laughed. The younger twin suddenly turned his buttocks to Jakpa and let out a loud, stinky fart. They roared with laughter.

Jakpa waited till they stopped laughing and the younger twin turned to say something, then he slapped him very hard on the cheek. The man opened his mouth in surprise, and Jakpa slapped him again, so that he closed it. Then he stepped back, tossing his bag to one side, and they were upon him. At first it was quite easy to dodge their wild angry blows, and he got in a number of painful punches to the noses and ears of his antagonists. But they were too much for him in the end. The elder twin feinted, and as Jakpa brought up his guarding arms he delivered a hard hook to the belly, and Jakpa gasped, and the fight went out of him. The elder twin pinned his arms behind his back, and the younger twin punched the helpless Jakpa in the face and the body. Jakpa suddenly brought up his legs and kicked out. The younger twin was knocked back several steps, and he covered his face with his hands. When he removed them his nose was one bloody pulp. He attacked madly, and this time the elder twin blocked Jakpa's legs with his, so that he was totally helpless. Jakpa felt his senses reeling.

A little crowd had gathered to watch the fight, but no one tried to interfere, possibly because of the reputation of the wild twins. Suddenly the main gate to Seku's home was opened, and Jakpa dimly recognised Seku himself standing there. He looked for a moment with surprise on his face, then he threw away his cloth and bounded into action. He grabbed hold of the younger twin who had drawn back his fist, and he twisted his arm and hurled him to the ground. The older twin protested angrily. He threw Jakpa aside like a sack of gari and he rushed at Seku. The two men exchanged a furious series of blows, and both staggered. The younger twin came and grabbed Seku from behind, and the elder twin hit him once, twice, in the stomach, then Seku made a sudden movement and the younger twin flew over his head magically. Again, he and the elder twin exchanged blows, then the elder Bawa sank slowly onto his knees and palms of his hands. The

87

younger twin dragged his painful body to his brother's side. The fight had gone out of them.

Seku went and helped his brother onto his feet, but as soon as he could stand Jakpa shook off his brother's hands feebly. Seku pretended not to have noticed and he addressed the inquisitive passers-by:

'Friends, why do you watch such a bloody fight without attempting to interfere? It was two against one, and the one man was my guest!'

The people shuffled their feet embarrassedly, then Seku said, 'Go, you cowards. Leave my sight, or I shall send for my gun to shoot your stupid heads off!'

The crowd dispersed slowly, and Seku turned to the Bawa twins. 'Who are you, miserable men?' he asked. 'Why do you waylay my guests in front of my own house? Speak, or we shall continue fighting!'

The elder Bawa scowled stubbornly, but the younger one said, 'Forgive us, honourable elder. We were only obeying instructions.'

'Instructions? Who gave you such outrageous instructions?'

'It was Opanin Yaw Ntiamoah, your friend. He paid us to prevent this man from attacking you.'

'Yaw Ntiamoah would never do this to me,' Seku shouted angrily. 'He would never tell you to kill this man. You are liars!'

'No, Opanin Seku,' said the younger twin. 'He told us not to kill him, but frighten him. Unfortunately he attacked us, and we had to hit harder than we originally intended.'

Seku looked at his brother, whose face was one bloody mess and whose white smock was torn and spattered with blood. He clenched his fists and ordered the twins, 'Go, get out of my sight! Never set foot in Aboabo again. If you should ever molest this man again, I shall castrate you with a sharp stone! Go!'

They got up and limped hurriedly away.

Seku cast his brother a look, glanced round and saw the leather bag lying nearby, and he went and picked it up. He said to his brother, 'Jakpa, you are hurt. Let us nurse you in my home.'

Jakpa shook his head proudly. He took a step and stood there shaking all over. His senses reeled, but he recovered with an effort and stood upright. He reached out an arm for the bag and Seku handed it to him.

'Jakpa, I didn't ask them to waylay you. I swear it. I shall have a talk with Ntiamoah, my friend. He is a good man, but he must learn that no one is to delay you in any way.'

Jakpa started to walk slowly away. Seku tried again to detain him: 'Brother, you are a nasty sight. Let me wash your face. You will

88

disgrace your good name walking to the palace like this. Come to my house, Jakpa.'

Jakpa faced him at last. He spat out a mixture of phlegm and blood, and said in a thick, barely audible voice, 'When I enter your house, Wattara, you will die. I go now, but I shall be back.'

Seku stood on the street looking after Jakpa, who never looked back. He remained there till long after Jakpa had gone, and when he went back home, he told his servant-bodyguards who had slept in their rooms throughout the encounter that they should tell the women to prepare no supper for him when they returned from the market.

7

The Mamponghene had finally arrived in the capital to assume power. He came with a large following, all in mourning cloths, late one evening, so that few people saw him. Some of the other Amanhene were already there, and the Mamponghene summoned all of them as well as the Kumasi chiefs to inspect the royal corpse. They held a long meeting, then the Mamponghene ordered the drummers to announce the news.

They drummed continuously till day-break, and still went on playing. The drummers of neighbouring villages heard the news and played the message on, so that the next day practically all those living in Asante knew. Otumfuor the adviser had 'travelled somewhere'; no more would the wise one give guidance as a living person. Osagyefo the redeemer was gone; no more would he defend the nation from her enemies. The mighty tree had fallen, and the birds had lost their nesting places.

Everywhere in Asante people donned their funeral cloths and rubbed ashes on their bodies. The various chiefs who could not go to Kumasi to see the body (because they were junior chiefs) caused their drums to be played offering condolence and promising to make the necessary sacrifices. The people wept loudly, and in Kumasi especially the situation was hysterical. Huge crowds gathered before the palace to weep and roll themselves in the dust. The abrafo and asafo warriors were like madmen. They kept out a watch to catch those not barefooted or in the proper mourning attire, and sometimes some of them suddenly fired off their guns and swung their swords wildly. People scattered before their approach, a few mourners were trampled to death, and one or two shot accidentally by the warriors.

In the place itself a butchery was taking place. A few slaves were being sacrificed to 'warm Otumfuor's soul' till the proper sacrifices could be made at the burial. The Gyaasehene took the king's favourite stool into the stool-house of the ancestors. As from that day the stool would be blackened with sacrificial blood at every Odwira festival, because even if Opoku II had ruled for only a few months, his soul would take its place with Nyame as a king of Asante.

Two days after the news was announced, Akosua went to the palace. It required great courage from her because of all the festivities taking place. One of the younger abrafo grabbed her hand at the gates and asked where she thought she was going. She had been weeping to show her sorrow at the news, and she answered in a broken voice that she had been sent by her uncle to visit Jakpa. The obrani smelled strongly of gin, but he was quite kind-hearted and led Akosua round the back of the palace to the little gate leading to Jakpa's courtyard. He explained that the main courtyard of the palace was for the benefit of only the senior elders till after the burial of the king.

Jakpa was sitting bare-chested on a stool before his rooms. He scowled when he saw Akosua and he turned his head away. But Akosua had already seen that his face was terribly swollen. One eye was closed, and the left side of the jaw was swollen. There was a cut under his closed eye. Akosua looked round, but apart from Kofi no other person was in the courtyard. She stood before Jakpa and said:

'I have come, Jakpa.'

He didn't answer at once, and she thought he hadn't heard, so she repeated what she had said. This time he replied:

'Yes, I see. Have you come to laugh and make fun of me? Have you come to see that I am beaten and suffering?'

Akosua held back her tears and said, 'I would never laugh at you, Jakpa. You know this, don't you?'

'Who told you to come? I didn't send for you.'

'I came of my own will, Jakpa. I heard what had happened, but I couldn't come earlier because of the announcement of the news, but I have managed it today.'

He didn't speak, but remained with his head bowed. Akosua went down on her knees and held his head gently with her hands. Jakpa made a half-hearted attempt to brush her off, but his face was like that of a little boy pretending to dislike something in reality he liked. Akosua said:

'The mother of one of my uncle's wives has come to visit her son-in-law. She is a herbalist, and I asked her for some of her cures. Please allow me to treat you.'

'I am all right,' he said gruffly.

But Akosua called Kofi and told him to fetch some hot water. When he brought it she poured out a small quantity into a calabash, undid her

91

waist-knot and took out some dried roots and leaves. She put some of them into the calabash. Kofi brought her a clean piece of cloth and she gently dabbed at Jakpa's face, which remained impassive throughout the whole operation. She saw that his left breast ached when touched, so she applied the treatment to his whole upper body as well. When she had finished she asked him if he felt better, and his scowling face relaxed a little as he nodded in reply.

She asked Kofi if his master had eaten before dawn, but he replied that for many days he had drunk only water. Akosua wanted to make him some soup, but of course she couldn't. If the abrafo found out, she would be beheaded immediately. Because of the royal death, no meals were allowed in the light of day.

She persuaded Jakpa to enter his rooms and lie down. She sat by his bedside and hummed songs to make him relax. He closed his one good eye and dozed lightly. She drew his cloth over him, and watched him with a feeling of peace in her. He suddenly opened one eye and said:

'You have come to tell me not to try again, eh, Akosua?'

She didn't answer.

'Well, you won't succeed. His thugs have beaten me up, but I shall keep on trying till I kill him. He is guilty, and more, he has further humiliated me. Imagine: I walked through town to the palace with bloodied clothes and a disfigured face.'

'They weren't his men,' Akosua said quietly. 'The men were working for his friend Ntiamoah, and Seku himself fought with them.'

'It doesn't change anything. How do you know this? Were you there?'

'I heard of it.' She shrugged.

'Think what you want, Akosua. I shall kill him.'

There was silence for a while. Akosua broke it saying, 'You lied to me, Jakpa.'

He looked at her, and in the puffy face she recognised a glow of embarrassment. He made no reply.

'You told me you hadn't yet seen your brother the day I came to see you after the funeral. In actual fact you had, in the very evening of the funeral. Then again you came to the market to warn me of the great passing away and you told me you would contact me before you approached your brother. I never knew you would ever lie to me, Jakpa, but you have done it. Why?'

'My sister,' Jakpa began, 'I didn't want you to worry about it. It is something I must do, and nobody must stop me, not even you.'

'You also made this promise,' Akosua went on as if he hadn't spoken. 'You said you would speak to my uncle about Nana Kuntunkuni, but you haven't done so. Do you care so little about my welfare? Does it not pain you to see me marry an old toothless man without your lifting a finger? I thought you had a heart, but now I see you are selfish and think only of yourself.'

'Akosua!' he sat up on his mattress, his hands held out in a pleading gesture. 'Akosua, please, I never forgot it. I really do intend to speak to your uncle about it, believe me. I have thought of all I shall say.'

'No, Jakpa,' she said with quiet finality. 'You think only of your priorities. You want to get yourself killed, and it doesn't matter two hoots to you how I live the rest of my life after you have gone.'

He stared for a moment then flared up: 'Woman, you want to use trickery to save Seku Wattara. I shall kill him! He is a dirty scoundrel!'

'You are no better than he, Jakpa. You tell me you hate how he betrayed your father, but you are just as hopeless. You work in the Otumfuor's palace, the same man whom your father hated!'

'I have never killed as Seku has done. My work here is passive.'

'No, Jakpa. Your documentation of events in Kumasi helps in a great way to give stability to the empire. You are just as effective as your warrior brother in keeping Asante strong.'

'Woman, you are Asante. Why do you tell me this to annoy me?'

'I am not trying to annoy you. I am just telling you that you aren't so angelic as you think. You are a fool, Jakpa.'

He got up at the insult, and she stepped back, expecting him to hit her. She picked up a broom nearby to defend herself. He stared at her, then sat down on his bed. When he spoke his voice was much more subdued:

'Perhaps you are right, my sister. Perhaps I am a fool. But sometimes a man must act foolishly if he wants to achieve something. I survived slavery by pretending to be stupid, and I have won the Imam's respect through my own respect and obedience to him. Perhaps if I had spoken harshly to him or some of the palace workers I would be headless now. Yes, I agree, I have been foolish in order to survive, and perhaps I must change now.'

'This is not what I meant,' Akosua said, not at all happy at his words. 'Jakpa, what will you do?'

He got up and folded his cover cloth, speaking as he worked, 'I shall do two things, Akosua. I shall kill my brother, then I shall approach the Kumasi elders and tell them my mind.'

'Jakpa, you are mad!' She stared at him, then ran to block the way out. 'I won't let you go. You must kill me, if you really want to die like this.'

He tried to push her out of the way, but she clung stubbornly to him. He saw that he was hurting her, and stopped. She lay her head on his shoulder and wept.

'I love you, Jakpa. I really do. I wish I didn't, but I think of you every time and every day. When I heard that you had been beaten at Seku's home, I stopped eating. If you let me go away knowing you will get yourself killed, today will be the third continuous day I haven't had anything in my belly. Have mercy on me, Jakpa. I love you so much.'

'I was just going outside, Akosua,' Jakpa told the sobbing girl. 'I can't fight Wattara sick like this, you know.'

She cried out, 'Don't let us talk of Seku, please. I think I shall go mad!'

He held her against his breast. Her head was right on his painful spot, but he didn't flinch. He very gently pressed his sore lips against her ear and blew into it. He said softly, 'Whatever happens, Akosua, remember that I love you very much.'

They stood in a tight embrace for several tender moments. Kofi rudely interrupted. He came in without knocking and said, 'My elder brother, the Imam is here.'

They separated and Jakpa made a clicking noise to show his displeasure at the manner of interruption they had been subjected to. A number of insults would have followed, but Kofi put a finger on his lips to show that the Imam would overhear them. Jakpa looked at the embarrassed girl, but she nodded for him to bring in his guest.

The Imam was not alone. With him was Ntiamoah. Jakpa was surprised, and Akosua's embarrassment increased. But his initial surprise rapidly evaporated and turned to anger, which he tried, as host, to contain. The Imam was shocked at Jakpa's swollen face, but he decided to make no comment on it because of the young man's pride.

They said the customary greetings, and Jakpa offered one of the two stools to the Imam. The other one he gave to Akosua, and when she made as if to offer it to Ntiamoah, he hissed sharply and she sat down. According to tradition Ntiamoah, and not the girl, should have got the stool. Ntiamoah pretended not to have been disturbed, but Kofi soon came inside with two more stools, so that everybody had a seat at the end.

Maalam Fuseini said, 'I know your story now, my son. I have finally

94

found out what has been troubling your mind. This kind man has told me everything.'

Jakpa and Ntiamoah exchanged looks. It was obvious that neither had much liking for the other. Jakpa said to the Imam: 'Has he also told you how he paid men to waylay me?'

Maalam Fuseini nodded patiently. 'He has since regretted it. His best friend rebuked him severely for doing it.'

Ntiamoah added, 'The Bawa twins have left town. Opanin Seku asked me to send them away and I obeyed. I offered them some gold dust to see to their safe journey to Dagomba, because I bear them no grudge.'

The words 'because I bear them no grudge' were clearly intended to annoy Jakpa. But Jakpa saw the man's game and decided to ignore his rudeness. He said, 'You are kind, Asante-ni. I bear them no grudge either.'

'My son,' said Maalam Fuseini, 'it is a strange thing, but we have worked together for several months, yet it is only today that I learn of your background. You do not know anything about my background either.'

'The Kramo is a well-informed and widely-travelled man,' Ntiamoah said. 'He knows Asante better than I, the nephew of a nobleman, and he knows and understands all her neighbours as if he had lived with them for many years.'

'I have seen and experienced a lot,' the Imam said. 'I have been to the north as far as Mamprusi and Mossi, to Kong, to Dahomey and to the coast. I have lived an interesting life. I have many memories in my head. The grasslands of the north, the forests of Asante and the plains at the coast. The dances and spears of the northerners, the guns of the southerners. I have even seen and visited the huge stone houses of the white men, and climbed aboard their great ships. They have wonders to display, these white men!'

He looked at Jakpa and said, 'Your father was the sort of man I respect. I had never heard of him but if what this young man tells me about him is true, then he was truly great.'

Jakpa glanced quickly at Ntiamoah, and began, 'My father hated slavery. He had no respect for men who sold off their subordinates as Asante sells human beings to the white men. His sons are not fit to follow in his footsteps.'

Ntiamoah muttered sarcastically, 'Perhaps you accuse your brother Seku. But you are no better than he, my friend.'

Jakpa stood up and said, 'I intend to change, Asante-ni. I shall kill my brother, then I shall denounce Asante before her own rulers. Mark my words, for this will surely happen.'

Maalam Fuseini asked quietly, 'Why must you kill your brother, my son?'

'Respectable Maalam,' Jakpa bowed a little as he spoke, 'my brother whom I loved and worshipped betrayed me. In addition he has ruined the good name of my father in Mossi.'

'You give two reasons,' the Imam remarked. 'Which of the two reasons is more important? Don't tell me they have the same importance, for that cannot be possible. One reason must always outweigh the other, even if by only a small margin. Be honest with yourself.'

Jakpa blinked his good eye at the unexpected question. He couldn't decide.

The Imam said, 'I shall put myself in your place. If my brother had betrayed me as yours did you, I would be filled with disbelief and hate. I would swear revenge, and I would struggle to survive with only one purpose in mind: revenge. Is this not what you always thought when you were in chains and naked, or when you laboured in a nobleman's farm?'

'It is the same,' Jakpa nodded vigorously. 'Every misfortune I underwent I always said "Seku" in my mind.'

'Then suddenly, after months and years of suffering, you suddenly met luck. You were freed from slavery, and you were given a very important post in a king's palace. You were liked by everybody who was in the palace, and you got a room, free, and some pocket money and a personal servant. You were assured that it could only get better for you: a house soon, then some land to farm, then even a chance to open a Moslem school. Tell me, my son, when all these things began happening, did you believe it was because of Seku?'

'No, never!'

'Whom did you remember? Who gave you the knowledge which saved your life and which earns you your daily meal? Was it not your father?'

Jakpa nodded, slowly.

'And what did you feel? Did you not feel gratitude for him for what he had given you? Did you not remember his ideals?'

'Yes, I did, and I do. I remember all that Baba expected of us, the

96

high ideals he set for us, and I feel regret and shame that I cannot fulfil his hopes.'

'If I were you,' the Imam said, 'I would especially hate Seku for ruining my father's name, for ignoring my father's ideals. Now tell me, my son: you have two reasons to kill your brother. Which reason is more important?'

The two men and the girl looked at the young man with swollen facial features. They held their breath, waiting for his answer. Finally Jakpa replied:

'My father was an idealist. He hated slavery and he continuously urged us to take interest in liberating Gonja if ever the opportunity arose. He was a good man respected by all, and he loved us his children. My memories of him are all tender. But my brother and I have deceived him. My brother broke away even while Baba was still living, and my love for him led me to help him later to steal a girl from the home of the very chief who had sheltered my father. Seku Wattara hurt me by betraying me, but more than that, he caused me to wrong my father in two ways: first, the people's memory of him in Kumbili is now without affection, and secondly, I have ended up serving the very same king I should attempt to overthrow. For this, he must die.'

'I understand,' the Imam said. 'I am glad you still remember your father with love and respect, and that you see that he was a very worthy man. I do not know the man, but I think you must have some of his qualities. You are the best Arabic scholar I have ever met, young as you are, and you have heart. I see this from how you live with Kofi, and in how politely and friendly a manner you comport yourself.'

'Seku keeps no slaves either,' Ntiamoah said defensively. 'Perhaps he also has some of his father's ideals.'

Jakpa got up to retort sharply, but Maalam Fuseini made a sign for him to sit again. 'I have a story to tell you, Jakpa,' he said. 'You know that I intend to write a book about Asante. I have collected many facts, and I believe they will be helpful in the future to all those who want to understand Asante and know how and why she is what she is. Before I begin, I want you to tell me something. Your father was a great scholar, and so I do not doubt that you know a lot of history. Now, where do the Gonja come from? Were they always where they are today?'

It was certainly a bit odd to switch from a case concerning death to one concerning historical knowledge. For a moment Jakpa stared in confusion, then he replied, 'The Gonja came originally from even

97

further north than they live today, to be precise they came from the far north-west just below the great river Joliba*.'

'Led by a great leader called Jakpa the Conqueror.' The Imam finished for him. 'Your father named you after him obviously in the hope that you would continue in his steps. Don't worry, you are still young. Now tell me also, where did the Mossi and Dagomba come from?'

'Originally from the north-east, near Hausaland. But Maalam, I do not think this moment is right to discuss tribal history. I have a case, and I am determined.'

'Patience, my son, patience,' The Imam turned to Ntiamoah: 'Now you, my young friend, tell us – where do the coastal Fante say they come from?'

'Originally from the north-west in the great plains. They were led to their present home by three chiefs called Oson (the "Elephant"), Odapagyan and Oburmankoma.'

'Good. Tell us again – the Brong live between Asante and Gonja. Do they have a history of migration similar to the Fante?'

Ntiamoah nodded. 'Yes.'

Maalam Fuseini went and touched Akosua's shoulder. He asked, 'What is the history of Asante, beautiful one? Where did the Asante come from?'

Akosua had been feeling quite relaxed so long as the men ignored her. Now she felt shyness growing in her, and she spoke quickly so as to get it over with and be freed of the attention of the men: 'From Asamankese. There was a great hole there, and our people came out of that hole.'

To Jakpa's surprise the Imam didn't show disappointment. He rubbed his hands together and said, 'Excellent. We shall come back to this. But let me ask Owura Ntiamoah again: where do the coastal Ga of Accra come from? Or the Ewe?'

'From the east. Some of them say they originally lived in the land of the Yoruba, and they were defeated and fled in canoes or even on foot along the coast.'

The Imam turned to face Jakpa. 'My son, many great events have happened in our land. There have been great migrations which sometimes took several decades to complete, perhaps even a century. That is a long time. Now I ask you: what important historical events occurred four or five hundred years ago? Or even before that?'

* Joliba is today's river Niger.

98

Jakpa didn't know what answer the man was expecting. He began uncertainly. 'There were many kings in Mali, and Ghana, some good, many bad. The Moslem religion began to spread —'

'Exactly,' the Imam interrupted. 'And how was Islam spread? Was it with peaceful methods as the Hausa used much later to convert the people of Dagomba or —'

'There were holy Jihads,' Jakpa answered. 'The Berbers conquered Mali even as in earlier times the Almoravids had destroyed Ghana. Mali had been Moslem for several centuries, but some of her subject states were not Moslem. The Berbers tried to change this by making it a capital offence not to worship Allah.'

'That is a reason for the migrations,' said the Imam. 'Many proud subject states refused to turn Moslem, and they chose to flee their land. The Berbers were unable to hold effective control for long, and soon Mali the great trading empire became a land of thieves and cut-throats. I am not saying that the Gonja and Fante and Ewe were once the same people. Even tribes not subject to the Malian court in Niani* had to flee as the escaping Malian tributaries approached with the intention of taking their land with force. Then came Askia Mohammed of Gao, one of the greatest rulers of Songhai. More conquests followed, and more migrations, because the people of Songhai preached Islam. Mind you, Jakpa, I haven't read this anywhere. It is just something I am putting together myself. The migrations of the Fante and Brong coincide with the destruction of Ghana in 1076, whereas the tradition of the Yoruba of Oyo says that the Yoruba originally lived in the plains, but they were pressured to move south into the forests, and the time they quote agrees fairly well with the time the Ga and Ewe say they were forced to flee that part of the world to their present location.'

The Imam was silent for several moments, as if he was giving someone a chance to ask something. But his three listeners were fascinated by his knowledge and waited for him to continue. Which he did:

'When you were new in the palace, my son, you told me that Jihads were good things. I believe in Allah, and I try to follow the Good Book, but I cannot agree that Jihads bring any good. Maybe elsewhere, but not in the land of black people. The people of Asante shrewdly avoid religious problems in their subject states, with the result that there are

---

* Niani was the usual capital of the Mali empire, not Timbuctu, as is often supposed today.

99

fewer migrations. But Jihads have brought only migrations and confusion in this part of the world.'

Jakpa said, 'It wasn't only Jihads, Maalam. It was drought and hunger as well. It is written that Kumbi Salleh, capital of Ghana, had green pastures. Today it is all desert.'

Maalam Fuseini nodded. 'True. But the important thing is, there have been migrations, and these migrations have been brought about by two causes: a natural cause, and the cause of the Koran.'

'It is Allah's wish,' Jakpa said solemnly. 'He works in strange ways.'

'I know. But it makes me sad, because these migrations resulted in confusion. Whole tribes and nations broke up into little bands, and there was war everywhere. The Fante conquered the Guans who originally lived in their land and they married their women and mixed with them, and I know that few true Guans survive to this day, and they consider themselves Fante or Akan.'

Jakpa asked, 'Is intermarriage not good, Maalam? It brings about unity and friendship.'

'Of course, I agree. But I think of the great migrations and the wars. There was confusion and mistrust everywhere, and people were filled with hate for one another. My son, your father was an outspoken man against slavery. Slavery is an old tradition in the world. There were slaves in old Ghana, Mali, among the Berbers, even in the land of Mossi. Did the Mossi not keep slaves while you lived there?'

'They did,' Jakpa admitted, 'but it is a different kind of slavery. A slave is regarded as a human being who can win his freedom. In Asante a slave is a thing. The Asante pride themselves on their just laws. They say that no man can take a life apart from the king's council of elders. But this law applies only to those people above common ranks. Slaves die in great numbers whenever a wealthy man dies.'

'Your father wanted to stop this sickness in his land. I hate it too, Jakpa, and I want it to stop. But I have one great disagreement with your father. He puts Asante at fault, but I see other greater forces.'

Jakpa stood upright proudly and cast a glance at his listeners before saying, 'It is Asante which has continually taxed all her many tributaries of men to sell as slaves. It is Asante which keeps on selling them because other men's blood is their source of income and power. Allah is not always just, for he should curse that their ignorant kings be forever sick and weak like Opoku II!'

'Jakpa!' Akosua stood up, her mouth open with fear. She looked at Ntiamoah anxiously. He had stood up, and he seemed greatly shocked. According to Asante tradition, it was taboo for anyone to insult the Asantehene. The punishment for this crime was death. Ntiamoah belonged to a family that was well respected in Kumasi, and he was bound by duty to report this, or even to give immediate punishment if there were eye witnesses to back his story up later. Ntiamoah seemed to be speechless, and his fingers shook. Even Maalam Fuseini was afraid. Finally, however, Ntiamoah said calmly:

'It would be wise for you to watch your words, young man. I love your brother, but I have my duties as well. I shall forgive this incident only once. If it ever happens again, I shall have no other choice but to report to the elders.'

He sat down, and the girl and old man sighed with relief. Maalam Fuseini made a mental note to persuade Jakpa later to make offerings of sheep before Ntiamoah as a sign of repentance.

Ntiamoah was speaking on, 'Young man, you accuse Asante of being slavers, but this is not fair. Not all of us have slaves. I keep no slaves, and I see slavery as a madness. And there are many better men than I who share this belief with me.'

The Imam said, 'I have come to beg you to continue your father's work: help me find an effective way out of this swamp. To do this, you must spare your brother.'

Jakpa shook his head. 'That I cannot do. He owes me a life.'

'I want you to remember this: your father loved you his sons, but he was prepared to sacrifice you for an ideal. If you had waged war against Asante you would surely have lost your lives. This your father knew, but he wanted you to try it. Remember that.'

Jakpa was silent.

'Slavery has changed, my son,' the Imam went on, 'and it has become like a flood in the plains – spreading without stop. We are all affected, Gonja, Fante, Dahomey or Asante. None of us can get out of it. Asante is as much trapped as Gonja.'

'The sons of Asante never climb aboard the slave ships, though,' Jakpa remarked sarcastically.

'Not today, perhaps, but once they did. I —'

Ntiamoah interrupted the Imam, 'Allow me, Kramo.' He turned to Jakpa, 'Once Asante was under Denkyera and was forced to sell many of her own people. At that time we lived in separate settlements. It was

101

the great Nana Osei Tutu who united us with the purpose of liberating ourselves from our masters.'

Maalam Fuseini said, 'Tell us, Yaw Ntiamoah: the Asante speak a dialect of Twi, the language of the Akan. The Fante and Brong are Akan with other dialects, and they have a similar history to each other. Why do the Asante say they came from a great hole?'

Ntiamoah glanced uncertainly at Akosua. She stood up obediently to go out, but Ntiamoah waved her back to her seat and said, 'My sister, I hope you will not tell this story to friends, because it will give me trouble.' She nodded readily and he said, 'Before Asante was first formed we fought against each other. Every village was for itself, and the union was very shaky in the beginning. Osei Tutu and his elders were afraid that this would weaken the effectiveness of the new nation, so they made it taboo for anyone to discuss the tales of migration and settlement in Asante. He and his advisers formulated the story of the great hole of Asamankese, which means the great hole of the great Spirits.'

'What were the tales of migration? Tell us why it was necessary to forbid discussion of these tales.'

'Well, while we were under Denkyera, we often robbed each other's villages in order to meet the quota of slaves demanded by Denkyera. We bore each other serious grudges, and this threatened our unity.'

'Even as the Gonja, Gyaaman, Akim, Brong, Wassa, Dagomba and countless others rob each other today to meet Asante's demands,' Jakpa remarked icily. 'But why should I believe you, Asante-ni? Maybe what you say is a fairy tale.'

Ntiamoah shook his head. 'No, it is not. Few people know this, and the secret is kept within tiny closed circles. If one of you here —' he looked at Akosua – 'should ever want to tell anyone of this, he shall have to ask me first. If I find out, it may be necessary for me to kill him, the one he informed, and myself. I know this story because one of my ancestors was Okomfo Tuda. He was the second most trusted fetish priest in Asante in the time of the formation of the Union, being exceeded in capability only by Anokye. He told the story to his favourite nephew, who passed it on. So far as I am aware, only three members of my greater family* know this secret. Neither of my parents know it.'

The Imam said, 'You do not know this, my son, but the Asante clans are the same as those of the Fante, Akwapim, Brong, or other Akan

* greater Akan family included sisters, cousins, uncles, parents, grandparents, etc.

tribes. I know for example that when Akwapim or Akim people of the Bretuo clan visit Mampon, they are called "brother". I do not know the origin of these clans, but it possibly has something to do with the great migrations, when people travelled in large companies.'

When he stopped speaking Ntiamoah addressed Jakpa, 'Okomfo Tuda was beheaded by the elders of Asante. After the mysterious death of Anokye, he became the nation's number one fetish priest. He was a hard-working man with sincerity and a powerful fetish, but he had no tact. He felt sick at heart as he saw that the Asante, after defeating Denkyera, had become slavers. He continually protested to the king and his elders, urging them to stop, but they wouldn't listen. Finally one day he went to consult his fetish. He was away for a long time, and when he returned he was like a wild man, dirty and with beady eyes. He went and sat in his humble hut and refused to eat or drink. When the chiefs heard of this, they persuaded the king to order the priest to tell them what his fetish had ordained, and there was a great durbar. It was Okomfo Tuda's greatest hour. He danced for a long time, then he waved his "bodua" of horsetail, and lo and behold! the sun disappeared behind some clouds and it began to rain. The chiefs took shelter under their giant umbrellas, but their attendants got very wet. Finally, Osei Tutu asked Okomfo Tuda to talk, and he bowed down before the king and said that he had heavy news. He reminded his audience that he had served them faithfully for many years, then he said that his message was simple. Asante had to stop the slave trade, or it would cause her downfall. The very white men who bought the slaves and made Asante rich would invade and burn Kumasi to ashes. The chiefs were aghast and felt insulted. Osei Tutu himself loved the man because he admired his honesty and courage, but his chiefs put extreme pressure on him, and to save the Union, he ordered Okomfo Tuda to be beheaded. They say that when the deed was done, only white powder, and not blood, was revealed in the man's neck. This is a hint that he had spoken the truth, and this is why I hate slavery.'

'My son,' the Imam said, 'Asante is as much trapped as Gonja with slavery. It is not they who hold the strings, but others.'

'Which others, Maalam?' Jakpa asked.

'Consider this, my son. When the white men first came to our shores, they met strife and confusion between our people, because of the great migrations. People were only too eager to sell them their neighbours who always stole their cattle and raped their women. Once it began, it couldn't stop.'

'Why not? Asante does not need to sell slaves to survive. Their land is far richer than that of the Gonja. They have water, fertile soils, gold in great quantities, and their craftsmen are noted for the beauty of their work.'

'It is easy to say that. You are young, you have never been to the coast to see the white men. They have wonders to show us. They build huge stone houses the like of which never existed anywhere in our world. Their ships are like huge floating castles, full of many rooms and with much food to last the numerous workers for months. Above all they have the gun, the supreme weapon. Asante gets her guns from them, but only in exchange for slaves. This is why Asante must sell men, so as to defend herself.'

'The people of Asante have many guns, collected over the years. They can stop the trade.'

'No, my son,' the Imam shook his head sadly. 'They do not have enough. And they need gunpowder and pellets, otherwise their guns are useless. Let me tell you a good reason why Asante should continue the trade. Once the people of Dahomey were under the Oyo empire. They were heavily sold off as slaves, and they suffered terribly. Finally they hit upon a desperate solution: they collected slaves from among themselves and sold them secretly to the whitemen at Whydah in exchange for guns. Let by a great general called Ajaja, they fought successfully to be free of Oyo. The Dahomeans had suffered terribly from slavery, and one of Ajaja's first actions after defeating Oyo was to extend his conquests to the coast at Whydah with the intention of closing the forts. For some years the Dahomeans enjoyed security and peace, then suddenly they suffered a severe defeat at the hands of the Oyo, whom they had once repelled. Many of them were sent to be sold. After this the Dahomeans got sense, and to this day they export more slaves than even Asante, for they have learnt the hard way that the gun is the supreme weapon.'

'Maalam,' Jakpa looked confusedly at him, 'you tell me you want me to help you stop slavery, but then you tell me in the same breath that it cannot be stopped. What shall I believe?'

'Then you want to stop this sickness?'

Jakpa nodded. 'I want to try. I remember my father's ideals. I want to work in the direction if it is possible.'

'Good. But the first step you must take is hard – let Seku Wattara live.'

Jakpa looked away, his shoulders shaking. 'I cannot do that,' he said.

'Besides, he will only undermine this. He cannot be trusted.'

'Jakpa,' Maalam Fuseini looked very sad. 'His is one life. You can save countless lives. Do you remember the Gyaaman War? Five thousand senior Moslems are under arrest. Probably they will be sold off to the white men, unless something happens to change the minds of the elders. Remember this: your brother is no Asante, but he is one of the most liked warriors in Kumasi. If he and I should approach the elders, I think we can influence them. I want you to know this: I am no small boy. I worked with Osei Kwadwo and we had mutual respect for each other. I worked with Osei Kwame at first very closely, but I recognised his evil mind and stopped giving advice and remained only a simple secretary, allowing Mumula and his friends to win his favour. I know I have the respect of the elders of Asante, and they will listen to me if I can use your brother's name to plead. This is why Seku must live.'

Jakpa looked away. He was very confused. He admired the Imam and he loved his father's memory, but he had sworn to kill his brother and he didn't want to turn back. Ntiamoah and Akosua looked anxiously at him, and Ntiamoah said:

'Your brother is the finest man I know, my friend. He could defeat you easily in battle, but he has told me he accepts his fault and will not lift a finger in his own defence. I wouldn't do this for my own father!'

Jakpa ignored him.

Maalam Fuseini said, 'I want to show you something, my son. It is something I have never displayed to anybody in Kumasi. I am old, and I know I shall soon die. I need someone to continue what I believe in. You are the most talented man I can trust, and if you turn me down, then it is finished.'

He began to undo the knots on his white smock. The three people looked at him in disbelief. Jakpa rushed to stop him and Akosua got up to go out. The Imam told them:

'My son, let me be. I must tell you who and what I am. Young woman, stay. You have heard great things today, it is fitting that you see something as well.'

Jakpa stood back, and Akosua remained where she was. The Imam finished undoing the knots and took off his smock and began to work on his under trousers. Ntiamoah watched him, fascinated, but Jakpa and Akosua looked away. The old man finished his work and dropped his trousers to the floor. He called Jakpa and Akosua to look, and they turned their faces slowly and unwillingly. Jakpa saw that Ntiamoah had buried his face in his hands and he hesitated, but the Imam called him and he looked.

The old man had a very thin body with the ribs showing. His muscles hung weak and flabby on his bones, and his knees appeared thicker than either thigh or calf. Jakpa moved his eyes slowly up the thin legs to the area of the groin, then he turned quickly away. Maalam Fuseini was an eunuch. And worse than that, his penis had been severed off near the end, leaving only a short stub.

The three of them looked away as the Imam began to dress up again. He got into his trousers, tightened the closing strings, then slipped into his smock. Akosua began to cry.

When he had finished, the old man said: 'I got this in Dahomey. I am a Kakri, Jakpa, I belonged to one of those small tribes which are constantly raided by all others to sell. The Dahomeans sent an expedition to depopulate my people, and I was one of those captured. I was not more than ten years old and I hadn't yet got tribal marks cut in my face. I was sent to the great castle at Whydah, and we were stored up in huge dark rooms under the castle and sent on board the ships of the white men, chained in long rows by our necks and legs, rather like animals. Here too we were led all the way into the damp dark cellars of the ships and forced to lie down in long rows next to each other. We ate and shat in the same space, and not surprisingly, some of us got ill. I was lucky to be one of them. I contracted a strange disease which made me shit water all day, and when they found out, they were alarmed. They dragged me to the top floor of the ship, removed my chains and threw me overboard. I was saved by some Dahomeans who took me home. They nursed me, and when I got better they fed me very well and would not let me work. After having lived with them for a few months, I found out why. One day I was told to follow the owner of the house and he led me into some thick forests till we came to a hut. Some fetish men were there: they suddenly grabbed hold of me, one of them prayed for a long time, and they cut away my manhood. It was probably to make a fetish against my master's enemies.'

'I was allowed to run away afterwards, because they were sure I would die. Luckily I met an old Dahomean lady, and she pitied me. She was a herbalist, and she applied her medicines, and when I was better, she took me to a Hausa trader passing through Whydah, and she explained that she had lost all her children through slavery and that she wanted to save me. The Hausa trader was a good man. He taught me all about the Holy Book, and since I had no other interest, I was his best pupil. I travelled with him for many years, for he was a merchant, and I learnt a lot. But one day he disappeared as well. It was again in Whydah and he told me he had been invited by a Dahomean elder who owed him. He never returned, and no one would tell us where he had gone, so we concluded that he had been sold as well. We feared for our own lives, and we dispersed. For many years I roamed through many lands. Sometimes I joined Hausa merchants, sometimes I went around with my own servants. I hated Dahomey and Whydah, and I pondered long over the problem of slavery. Once it occurred to me to visit my home village in Kakri to see if I would recognise any of the survivors there. But I met a caravan of chained slaves led by Dagomba warriors, and I couldn't bear the thought of continuing my journey to see the burnt remains of what the slavers had left behind. I prayed and fasted, and I asked Allah to give me strength to find a solution. My son,' he looked at Jakpa, 'like you I had blamed the very people who punished me, the Dahomeans, but after I had seen the Dagombas I grasped the real cause. It is the white men. They are taking advantage of the hate we feel for each other to make us sell ourselves. Believe me, if Asante stopped selling slaves, other people would be given guns and the sickness will continue.'

Now there was silence in the room. Jakpa stood with bowed head, the girl and Ntiamoah were looking at the old man. Outside the drummers were beating their message, and they had been joined by the horn blowers. Occasionally, a gun was fired off, and there were many songs of woe sung by the women of Kumasi.

Maalam Fuseini spoke on, 'I came to Kumasi with many presents and things to sell. I did a lot to win the trust of Osei Kwadwo, Asantehene, and I was the first Moslem commissioned to write down records of Asante. I had to overcome my disgust for some of their habits: human sacrifice, mutilation of humans for the least offence, the warlike nature. It is strange, but even Asante's cruelty is a sign of her own fears. Other Akans do not make human sacrifice or take so much pleasure in bloodshed and torture. It is something that the slavers indulge in. Oyo and Dahomey are even more bloodthirsty than Asante, and when Denkyera ruled Asante, she acted the same way. I am telling you all this, Jakpa, so that you will recognise that you have power which you could use well. I have worked my way into the trust of the rulers of Asante, and you should be my successor and continue my work. I have only one simple plan: unity. Let us all unite, then there will be no need for us to sell ourselves for guns to defend ourselves from our own brothers. Defeating Asante will only make the new conquerors slavers themselves. If on the other hand we can unite peacefully, then my people the Kakri will finally have peace.'

He sat down, tired by his long speech. Jakpa asked him quietly, 'How do you plan unity, Maalam? It will need many years.'

'True, my son. But one step at a time. For many years I have worked hard to gain the trust of Kumasi. I think the time is ripe for one further step. I remember the prisoners of the Gyaaman War. They can be saved by you, me and your brother the trusted warrior. They are over five thousand, and your brother is only one life.'

Ntiamoah said to Jakpa, 'We have seen great things today. I beg of you, remember your own father and consider the respectable Kramo who began serving in the palace before you were born. Let your brother live.'

Akosua went and took Jakpa's hand in hers. 'Do as they say, Jakpa,' she said simply.

Jakpa stood looking at the floor. Maalam Fuseini got up and went to look outside. He addressed Akosua, 'Young one, it is getting late. We mustn't forget that the king of Asante is dead, and that his warriors are wild. I propose that all three of us take you home.'

Akosua nodded obediently. Jakpa went into his sleeping room and put on his smock. They stood up when he joined them and the Imam said:

'I shall not ask you again, my son. I know you need time to think over what I have said. Do as you believe is right.'

They stepped into the little courtyard and left the palace through the back gate. They wanted to avoid the main crowd of mourners before the front gates, so they chose a narrow path through some woods. It was late afternoon and the sky was red as if stained with blood.

8

Market day, but one with a difference. It was the first permitted day of public selling of food since the announcement of the Great Passing Away. There weren't as many people there as normally came, and all those who did come were in mourning cloths. Discussions and bargaining were conducted in subdued voices, and some articles were even given away and not sold by the market-mammies as a sort of commemoration of the event in the palace. There were numerous red-eyed abrafo and asafo men standing in various places of the markets with folded arms. Only the crows and strong-beaked vultures gathered round the butchers' quarters seemed their natural selves and engaged in vigorous competition with each other for cast-away meat. Even the mongrels of the markets could sense the people's tension and accordingly avoided too much obvious stealing.

In Akosua's stall there was much less to sell than was usual; one had to be careful not to sell so much as to arouse the suspicion of the elders that one wanted to make profits at this solemn period. Even those who ventured to buy in the markets bought only little to display their lack of greed.

Maame Ntosuor looked again at Akosua. She had been excited all morning, often standing up to look through the rows of stalls around her. She had been behaving strangely ever since the time of the late Lady Mbinge's accident, and she had become very secretive in her ways. The old lady knew, or strongly suspected, her love for Jakpa, and since she herself liked the young man, she had connived at her meetings with him, but now she began to ask herself if she was doing the correct thing. Nana Amoaten would hardly be pleased if he found out that his niece had been meeting a man in secrecy behind his back. Today, too, on the very first market day in weeks, the young woman seemed to be waiting for someone.

'Akosua,' the old lady began uncertainly, 'be careful. If you should get a belly ...'

Akosua's look stopped her. She seemed very annoyed. 'We don't play such games, Nana. I am not a fool. Besides there is another matter more important than mere love.'

'I hear you,' the old woman said meekly.

Akosua could sense her quiet disbelief and it vexed her. 'Nana, he is going to see someone with me today. It is a very important occasion, but I can't tell you everything now.'

'Hmm.' Maame Ntosuor didn't seem much convinced, but to avoid angering Akosua further, she put a chewing stick into her mouth and busied herself with cleaning her teeth.

The only maid who had accompanied Akosua and Maame Ntosuor said, 'Jakpa is coming,' and both Akosua and the old woman forgot their quarrel and looked up expectantly.

Jakpa was quite near, and with no thick crowds to delay him he soon reached the stall and said his greetings. Akosua was glad to see that his face was much better already and he had both eyes open to the light of day, but Maame Ntosuor, who hadn't seen Jakpa for days, was shocked.

'My son!' she exclaimed, standing up. 'What has happened? How did your handsome face get like this?'

In the unusual silence of the market her words carried far, and some of her neighbours came to find out the matter.

Jakpa was embarrassed by the presence of so many strange females, and so he lied, 'I fell into a bees' nest, Nana.'

'Bees?' The old woman was standing with her hands on her hips. 'Do bees cause such wounds and swells?'

She came forward and felt his face and neck, and her neighbours too came and did the same, and they chattered and chattered. Luckily for Jakpa some of the asafo saw the spectacle, and the women dispersed quietly before the warriors lost their temper. Jakpa now confessed to the old woman that he had been waylaid by some thugs.

'Thugs! Nyame! AND I didn't know! Tell me, my son. Who were they, where was it, and were they caught? Did they rob you?'

Jakpa would have preferred not to discuss the matter any further, but Maame Ntosuor was insistent, and at last he said, 'They were caught and have been punished. They didn't rob me but succeeded in beating me up very cruelly.'

'Nyame is kind, my son. See how he spares good men like you. Akosua,' she turned, 'why didn't you tell me? I know you have often been to see him in the past few days, when the Great Passing Away confined us all to our homes except at weeping times. You have been very secretive of late. Don't just stand there, talk!'

Jakpa came to Akosua's rescue and tried to change the topic by asking about Nana Amoaten, his wives and children. They were all fine, he was told. He also asked about the maids and servants and Maame Ntosuor replied:

'The maids who are home are all fine. Has Akosua told you? One of them is suckling the baby of our late friend . . . and Owura Seku and his friends have got Nana Amoaten's permission for her to stay in his house for a few months till the child can live on normal food alone. She often visits us, so we don't miss her so much, except now during the funeral festivities. Owura Seku is a fine man, and none of us doubts that he will look after her well.'

Jakpa replied that Akosua had informed him of this, and Maame Ntosuor said:

'Then it is good. But I don't think you know this, because you haven't seen her for three days. Gyima is back. He was in his village, and he has seen that he has better chances with Nana Amoaten's farm. The memories of the times he had lived there won't permit him to settle down again peacefully.'

Gyima had been the senior-most servant of Nana Amoaten's home for seven years, and soon after Jakpa had left the house, he had got permission to go home to his village, as his term of bondage was over. Jakpa hadn't seen him for months, but they had learnt to like and respect each other during the time they had lived and worked together, and he expressed his gladness to hear the news and promised to call at Nana Amoaten's specially to see his old friend.

'You remember the story I told you months ago?' Maame Ntosuor asked. 'Gyima became a slave because he couldn't pay his uncle's funeral debts, and during his years as a slave he lost his wives, farms and home. Now his favourite wife is wedded to the village chief, and he feels he can't live there with them. Luckily Nana Amoaten is now offering him land so long as he manages his big farm for him. Women are disgusting sometimes. Gyima is a simple, honest man, but he was so naive as to believe that his wife would keep her promise to wait for seven years. Now he knows better.'

'Men are no better,' Akosua cut in, and both Jakpa and Maame Ntosuor laughed.

'I agree, my daughter,' Maame Ntosuor said. 'In these hard times one has to tread carefully because there are few true friends in existence.'

They sat there for a while in silence, each with their own thoughts, then Maame Ntosuor said, 'Akosua tells me you are taking her somewhere. She won't tell me where, but wherever that is, promise to take care. Akosua is no common girl.'

Jakpa was embarrassed. Akosua called sharply, 'Nana!' but Jakpa began speaking before she could continue, 'I have no irresponsible intentions towards her, Nana. If you like she can stay behind for me to go alone.'

'Where are you going?'

'To see my brother. He lives in Aboabo.'

'It is far.'

'Nana,' Akosua began, 'he had a dispute with his brother, and wants to make his peace. It would be good if he would not go alone.'

'Is that so?' Maame Ntosuor looked at Jakpa. She found nothing strange about hearing of Jakpa's brother because she knew that to most northern strangers in Kumasi, any person from the same village, town or even state was a 'brother', and she also knew that there were several Gonja in Kumasi.

Jakpa confirmed that it was so.

'Then it is good,' the old lady said, 'I trust you, my son. I know you won't take her to a place where she will get into trouble. Forgive me for being so nosy this day, but Akosua has reached marrying age, and we are looking for a husband for her.'

'I understand, Nana.' Jakpa exchanged looks with Akosua. She waved him away in a childish gesture and looked elsewhere.

'Of course,' Maame Ntosuor went on, 'we want only the best for her. It must be someone of respectable family background, or with some respectable position in the society. Respectable people also want respectable wives. This is why I worry about how you move with Akosua. When a mango fruit pleases you, you eat all of it, because if you suck only a little, nobody else wants the rest and the magnificent fruit will be wasted. Tell me frankly, Jakpa, does this mango please you?'

Jakpa felt too shy to answer directly. Both Akosua and the silent maid were looking elsewhere, but it was easy to see that their ears were not turned to any other conversation than that between him and the old woman. 'I am only a small boy,' he ventured. 'I have no family in Kumasi, and I have risen from slavery.'

'No, my son. You are a boy in years, but your head is certainly mature and intelligent. No matter how my people may condemn reading and writing as a past-time for weak men, you have a power which even the king and his elders lack and respect. Certainly you are a respectable citizen of Asante by all standards, even if you were once used as a common slave. That is over and a bright future awaits you. If I may tell you a secret, I know Nana Amoaten will not object to having you as a son-in-law.'

Jakpa's eyes had a glimmer of hope, but he remembered and he glanced at Akosua before he spoke, 'You flatter me, Nana, but I know that a highly respectable citizen has already begun making his marriage arrangements.'

'You mean that old Kuntunkuni?' She laughed. 'Nana Amoaten turned him down. He said the girl was already promised to someone.'

Jakpa glanced at Akosua. She had been pretending not to hear the discussion, but he thought he could discern a faint mocking smile on her lips, and he had to control his annoyance and turn his attention to Maame Ntosuor.

'I assure you she is free,' the old woman went on. 'Many men want her, but her uncle wants someone with influence at the king's court. Think about it, Jakpa. She will make a fine eldest wife.'

Jakpa assured her he would, and he thanked her for telling him so much. He then begged leave to go, and Akosua accompanied him from the stall. When they were out of earshot he turned to her furiously and said:

'Akosua! You didn't tell me your uncle turned down old Kuntunkuni.'

She replied calmly, 'You never asked. You seemed preoccupied with your own troubles.'

'Come, you foolish girl. You made me promise to see your uncle, and imagine my foolishness if I had approached him.'

'But you didn't.'

'I intended to go this very afternoon. I have asked the Imam advice on how to approach your uncle. I have even bought a goat for him. I have practised what I wanted to tell him. Now it seems all the time has been wasted for nothing. Why in Allah's name did you keep me believing that you and that old Kuntunkuni were going to get married? Why did you come to me in the first place if your uncle had already turned him down?'

'My uncle didn't turn him down completely the first time. He said that I was already promised to someone, but he said he would talk to that person, and since I was sure it was only a trick to force a bigger bride-price, I came to ask you to speak to my uncle.'

'But you forgot to tell me that the matter was settled. Who are you promised to, anyway?'

'There was nobody.'

'Nobody?' He raised his eyebrows. 'Well then, how did your uncle make Kuntunkuni believe him?'

'It is over. Is it so important that you know?'

They had now left the market and were by the main street leading to Aboabo. Jakpa held Akosua's shoulder and made her face him.

'Don't play with me, Akosua. I am serious. Who is it? Why did Maame Ntosuor tell me your uncle liked me?'

She was looking at him with a mischievous smile. 'Do you like me, Jakpa?'

His eyes seemed to bore into hers. She saw the tensed muscles of his face. But he was not angry, just emotionally moved. He choked over the words, 'I have told you I love you, Akosua. Some time ago I was ready to die for a cause, but now I have been convinced it would be better if I lived. Some time ago I completely shoved aside any hopes or desires to wed you, but today you are one thing I must have. If I should lose you I might as well leave Kumasi. The Imam and his ideas can go ablaze. I have many memories to remember of this town to haunt me all my days: human butchery, my times as a slave, my brother Seku and Mbinge the beautiful. Today Seku and I shall be reconciled, but this compensation will not be enough to keep me in the palace. I must have Akosua Kyem as well. Now tell me – to whom has your uncle promised to marry you?'

Akosua was looking down with happy, down-cast eyes. At his question she took his hand in hers and said, 'It is nobody, my Kramo. I underestimated my uncle in believing he would give me off to Nana Kuntunkuni. He couldn't turn down such an important man directly, so he invented the story of my suitor. Honour forbade the proud warrior to ask who he was, which would have made my uncle feel very embarrassed. He has told me before his wives and Maame Ntosuor as witnesses that he has found nobody as yet.'

Jakpa squeezed her hand till it hurt. He smiled down at her and said, 'I think I shall talk to the Imam about you and your uncle. He can name whatever bride-price he wants, for I know that both the Imam and my brother will back me up.'

They were looking at each other for what seemed ages, holding hands. There were few men on the Aboabo street, and most were red-eyed asafo warriors. They were in their characteristic loin cloths, barefooted as usual in the red, wet earth of Kumasi. The sky was

114

fiercely hot. On either side of the street were houses, but not so densely packed together as in other parts of Kumasi, and there were green carpets of grass, with the tall green trees in the distance. Kumasi seemed very beautiful as they walked down the street.

Jakpa's mind was full of many thoughts. He was happy about what he had heard in the market place, because he truly loved Akosua and was convinced that she would make an excellent eldest wife. But as they approached Aboabo his mind gave more consideration to his brother whom he had once sworn to kill. His face betrayed none of his inner feelings, but Akosua could sense his increasing nervousness as they walked, and she asked no questions. Jakpa said to himself, 'Seku, my brother, you who strayed from Baba's rigid lines of discipline, you who have shamed my father's name among those who saved him, you who betrayed the love I had for you, to you I come to make peace. I have had many bitter thoughts about the things you did to those who loved you, but now I want peace. You have been punished by your own conscience for years, a guilt which will pursue you all your life. You will remember the evil you did your parents, you will remember that the woman you loved most of all was killed by an enemy of yours before her time. You will make your peace with me, but the others you harmed, you can never see them again till your death, and it will haunt you. But we are brothers, Seku, and Allah knows that I still remember the love we felt for each other. On my part I pledge the deepest peace, a near return to our days of mutual love. I pledge that I shall continuously try to set your conscience at ease. We shall try as best as we can to continue Baba's struggle, even if a bit differently from what he had originally planned. We both have some respect among our hosts, together we can help steer Asante from the cruel path of slavery, we can serve our devastated Gonja nation by striving to make Asante aware of the danger which her own fetish priest Tuda once predicted. The way for us all is unity.'

Aboabo, the white-washed houses, the last house in Aboabo before the jungles of Asante began. Two men were standing in the doorway. As they came nearer, one of them walked to meet them, and Jakpa recognised Seku. He looked hollow-eyed with lack of sleep and he wore a sad smile which betrayed his uncertainty. The two brothers stared silently at each other for several moments and embraced. Seku led the way inside, Jakpa following with Akosua bringing up the rear. Ntiamoah closed the gate. Outside, the birds sang cheerfully, as if unaware that all Asante was in mourning.

EPILOGUE

It is recorded history that when Osei Tutu Kwame became King of Asante in 1807, Asante policy began to come into serious conflict with that of the British and other Europeans. By this time the British had become the most important European power in a small area of coastal central West Africa, and they had begun to dream of empires bigger than the Roman. They cleverly worked up strong feelings of resentment in many coastal states subject to Asante and armed them with guns and tried to build them up as a united front against Asante. In 1824, the British Governor at Cape Coast received shiploads of British soldiers, and together with Fante troops they attempted to storm Kumasi. They failed, but the battle cost Asante the life of her king Osei Tutu Kwame, who only a few years before had been nicknamed Osei 'Bonsu', the 'whale', conqueror of the coastal Fante. MacCarthy, the British leader, was beheaded and his head taken to Kumasi as a war-trophy.

History again shows that Osei Bonsu tried to bind Asante's northern tributaries more closely to Asante. Some of the many rebels he pardoned included the five thousand Moslems of Gyaaman, which had rebelled against Asante rule during the time of his predecessor Osei Kwame. The Moslems were neither beheaded, enslaved nor stripped of their property, but they were scattered in little bands all over Asante to 'learn Asante customs'.

But history does not give the full reasons for these changes. History does not pay much attention to the fact that most of the king's Moslem secretaries came from the conquered north which supplied Asante's slaves. History pays attention only to Asante's activities in the south; few historians even know today that in the later years, many of Asante's greatest warlords came originally from the conquered north. The conquered ones were learning very fast that the final way out of the web of slavery would be to unite. Nobody knows today that once there was an old Kakri Imam in the palace of the Asantehene who clearly saw this way as the best, and that he had a young man trained to carry on his beliefs.

But it would be incorrect to say that slavery was completely stopped by Asante. Indeed, after the death of Osei Bonsu, Asante became very much aware of the intentions of the whitemen. Slaving was increased in the hope of obtaining more guns, and it is recorded that when the whitemen decided to stop slavery, Asante, economically crippled, declared war on the British, which finally led to the destruction of Kumasi in 1874, and a final crushing of Asante in 1900.

Jakpa was the king's head secretary at the time of the 1824 War. Maalam Fuseini had died ten years before, to be accorded a respectable burial attended even by the king himself. Jakpa was glad he wasn't alive to see Asante's narrow victory which confirmed his belief that the whitemen's intention all along was the final conquest of the blackman, and he was also glad that the old man would be spared from seeing the frantic efforts of Asante after 1824 to sell more and more slaves for guns.

Seku fell in battle at the king's side. By this time, he had assumed the Asante name Kwame Amirika (the 'Runner'), and he was one of Asante's most trusted generals. A young survivor said later that in the final stages of the fight, some of the British warriors unexpectedly walked into the king's retinue, which was at the far back of the army. Both sides were surprised, because the British themselves were fleeing. There were panicky shots from both sides, and the king was killed in the jungle: Seku had thrown his body across the king's a moment too late, but he was hit in the chest and died after firing only one shot, which hit a well-dressed European in the neck. The Europeans were all killed, as were their Fante followers, by the Gyaase regiment, which came to the rescue. The Asante were greatly saddened by the death of their king, but upon inspecting the dead Europeans they found a compensation: the one man Seku had shot was the British Governor himself. The Asante did not pursue the fleeing remnants of the British army, but turned to Kumasi to make a big funeral for the king and their brave warriors. Seku was one of the generals most mourned.

Seku's son was by this time growing into a young man, with all the women eyeing him. He was so shocked by his father's death that Jakpa ordered him to come and live with him for some months. Jakpa's wives, four in number now, took good care of him, but none was as comforting as Akosua, the first wife, whom the young man had long considered as second mother. He was an intelligent man, gentle and polite to the elders, but full of courage. His uncle taught him Arabic and was obviously interested in promoting him over his own sons as a possible heir to the job of record-keeper. The young man would never know that whilst he was still a baby, this same uncle had so nearly killed his father. Perhaps it was better so.

This then, is the story of Seku and Jakpa. But it is also the story of Maalam Fuseini, and of Africa in one of the most trying periods on human record.

GLOSSARY

ABRAFO   Place executioners (plural form).

ADAE   A festival to honour the ancestors, held once every three weeks.

ASAFO   Warriors of certain divisions.

ASANTEHENE   King of Asante.

ASANTENI   Citizen of Asante.

AWURAA   Lady, madam.

BANTAMAHENE   Chief of Bantama, a suburb of Kumasi. Among his duties as 'mayor' of Kumasi was to command Kumasi's soldiers in the confederal army. The post was not hereditary and usually went to a deserving warrior.

BEKWAIHENE   Chief of Bekwai state.

BODUA   Magic whisk of horsetail.

DYULA OF KONG   King of Kong, a Moslem state independent of Asante.

−FO   People, citizens.

FON OF DAHOMEY   King of Dahomey, a rival state.

GYAASEHENE   Chief of finance and palace matters. The post was not hereditary.

GYASE REGIMENT   A rear regiment which formed the personal guard of the senior-most commanders.

−HENE   Chief, king.

KABA   West African 'blouse'.

KAMBONSE   Frontal regiment of the Asante army, with recruits mainly from the conquered north.

KENTE   Most prestigious cloth in Asante society, woven of threads of many colours. Certain designs were reserved only for the King and the senior-most chiefs, and it was a crime for ordinary citizens to wear these.

KOBIN   Red funeral cloth.

KOKOA   Wrestling art of the sahel area of West Africa.

KRAMO   Akan word for a Muslim.

KUNTUNKUNI	Black funeral cloth.
KYENKYEN CLOTH	Cloth beaten from the bark of the kyenkyen tree, and often used for burial pupsoes. The Asante used no metal or wooden coffins.
MAAME	Mother.
MAMPONGHENE	Chief of Mampong town, and second most important man in Asante after the King. Commander-in-Chief of the Asante army.
MAUSOLEUM	A century after the setting of this story, the Mausoleum in Bantama (see page 81) was blown up by invading British soldiers. Baden-Powell (founder of the Boy Scout Movement) wrote that it made a great fire.
NANA	Grandparent, title of respect.
NYAME	God Almighty.
−NI	Person, citizen.
NKONTOMIRE	The large soft leaves of the cocoyam plant. It tastes like spinach.
OBRANI	Palace executioner (singular).
OHENE	Chief, king.
OBONSAM	Satan.
OKOMFO	Fetish priest.
OPANIN	Elder, title of respect.
OSAGYEFO	Redeemer, title reserved only for the Asanthene.
OTUMFUOR	Advisor, title reserved only for the Asantehene.
OWURA	Mister.
PIETO	Pants.
SEPO	Death by torture.

Yaw M. Boateng was born in Kumasi, Ghana, in 1950. Educated in Ghana and Cape Coast, he holds a master's degree in civil engineering from the Swiss Federal Institute of Technology in Zurich. He has written a number of plays and short stories, including the historical play *Katier,* which was performed on television in Ghana in 1972.

The Return is Yaw Boateng's first novel.